A HUNT OF FIENDS

A SHADE OF VAMPIRE 53

BELLA FORREST

Series 1: Derek & Sofia's story

A Shade of Vampire (Book 1)

A Shade of Blood (Book 2)

A Castle of Sand (Book 3)

A Shadow of Light (Book 4)

A Blaze of Sun (Book 5)

A Gate of Night (Book 6)

A Break of Day (Book 7)

Series 2: Rose & Caleb's story

A Shade of Novak (Book 8)

A Bond of Blood (Book 9)

A Spell of Time (Book 10)

A Chase of Prey (Book 11)

A Shade of Doubt (Book 12)

A Turn of Tides (Book 13)

A Dawn of Strength (Book 14)

A Fall of Secrets (Book 15)

An End of Night (Book 16)

Series 3: The Shade continues with a new hero...

A Wind of Change (Book 17)

A Trail of Echoes (Book 18)

A Soldier of Shadows (Book 19)

A Hero of Realms (Book 20)

A Vial of Life (Book 21)

A Fork of Paths (Book 22)

A Flight of Souls (Book 23)

A Bridge of Stars (Book 24)

Series 4: A Clan of Novaks

A Clan of Novaks (Book 25)

A World of New (Book 26)

A Web of Lies (Book 27)

A Touch of Truth (Book 28)

An Hour of Need (Book 29)

A Game of Risk (Book 30)

A Twist of Fates (Book 31)

A Day of Glory (Book 32)

Series 5: A Dawn of Guardians

A Dawn of Guardians (Book 33)

A Sword of Chance (Book 34)

A Race of Trials (Book 35)

A King of Shadow (Book 36)

An Empire of Stones (Book 37)

A Power of Old (Book 38)

A Rip of Realms (Book 39)

A Throne of Fire (Book 40)

A Tide of War (Book 41)

Series 6: A Gift of Three

A Gift of Three (Book 42)

A House of Mysteries (Book 43)

A Tangle of Hearts (Book 44)

A Meet of Tribes (Book 45)

A Ride of Peril (Book 46)

A Passage of Threats (Book 47)

A Tip of Balance (Book 48)

A Shield of Glass (Book 49)

A Clash of Storms (Book 50)

Series 7: A Call of Vampires

A Call of Vampires (Book 51)

A Valley of Darkness (Book 52)

A Hunt of Fiends (Book 53)

A Den of Tricks (Book 54)

A SHADE OF DRAGON TRILOGY

A Shade of Dragon 1

A Shade of Dragon 2

A Shade of Dragon 3

A SHADE OF KIEV TRILOGY

A Shade of Kiev 1

A Shade of Kiev 2

A Shade of Kiev 3

THE SECRET OF SPELLSHADOW MANOR

(Completed series)

The Secret of Spellshadow Manor (Book 1)

The Breaker (Book 2)

The Chain (Book 3)

The Keep (Book 4)

The Test (Book 5)

The Spell (Book 6)

BEAUTIFUL MONSTER DUOLOGY

Beautiful Monster 1

Beautiful Monster 2

DETECTIVE ERIN BOND (Adult thriller/mystery)

Lights, Camera, GONE

Write, Edit, KILL

For an updated list of Bella's books, please visit her website: www.bellaforrest.net

Join Bella's VIP email list and she'll send you an email reminder as soon as her next book is out: www.forrestbooks.com

NEW GENERATION LIST

- **Avril (vampire):** adopted daughter of Lucas and biological daughter of Marion.
- **Blaze (fire dragon):** son of fire dragons Heath and Athena.
- **Caia (part fae/human):** daughter of Grace and Lawrence.
- **Fiona (vampire):** daughter of Benedict (son of Rose and Caleb) and Yelena.
- **Harper (sentry/vampire):** daughter of Hazel and Tejus.
- **Scarlett (vampire):** daughter of Jeramiah (son of Lucas Novak) and Pippa (daughter of Cameron Hendry).

FAMILY TREE

If you'd like to check out the Novaks' family tree, visit:
www.forrestbooks.com/tree

1

HARPER

(DAUGHTER OF HAZEL & TEJUS)

With a face on our enemy and Fiona missing, our entire mission on Neraka had just taken a much more dangerous and urgent turn. Not that it had been breezy or stress free before, but the stakes were suddenly higher, as it wasn't just about the lives of innocent Maras and Imen anymore. Fiona's predicament, abducted by a daemon and most likely taken to the Valley of Screams, took center stage.

We all stood in our part of the infirmary, with the side door leading to other rooms boarded up and sealed, and the front door heavily guarded by Correction Officers. Minah and the daemon's body were under the same preservation and protection spell as we went over all the known facts, the many questions we still had, and our options moving forward.

"There are just so many things wrong with this picture." Heron sighed. "I never expected it to get this complicated."

"Our priorities are clear, though," Hansa replied, her gaze fixed on the dead daemon's face. His horns poked out from his thick black hair, sharp, their tips slightly reddened from the flesh they must've torn through over the years. "We need to get Fiona back, first. We'll then return here, send one of us back to Calliope, and find out what the hell they're doing with that prison. There are hundreds of Maras and Imen still missing, and daemons lurking around, eager to nab more."

"She must be somewhere in the Valley of Screams," I said, remembering Minah's account of her capture. "What do the maps we have say about cave formations in those gorges?"

"A few have been noted, but only with estimates of depth and length," Avril replied, moving closer to the maps spread out on the table close to Patrik's bed, along with our journals and the handful of scrolls I'd nabbed from the Exiled Maras' library. "There is a higher number of them through one specific gorge, though I'm not sure how much of a difference that will make. We will be following the tracking spell for Fiona, but we need to know what to expect from whatever route it takes us through, and the safest and fastest way out, once we retrieve her."

"Okay, Avril, can you and Jax help set possible exit routes?" Hansa asked, then looked my way. "Harper, go summon the Five Lords, please. They need to see the face of their enemy."

One of them already has, I thought to myself, remembering my earlier encounter with Caspian.

I nodded and left the infirmary. It was close to one in the morning, and all three moons were still out, glowing softly against the black sky. The six Correction Officers posted outside were staring out toward the Valley of Screams, their hands behind their backs. They were dressed in dark brown and gray, a blue badge sewn onto each right arm—they weren't meant to draw attention when scattered through the crowds, but they sure had mine right now.

I stopped in front of them, then moved closer to one, until he couldn't help but look me in the eyes for a brief moment before resuming his empty stare. I was angry and had way too many question marks hovering over my head— did they know about Caspian and his masked endeavors? What were they doing in that prison? Why did they let the daemons in to attack the inmates?

"We found your prison," I said, but the Mara kept a straight face. "One of the gates opened at midnight, and let daemons in to feed on the prisoners. Is it something you people do on purpose? Is that what happens to those who oppose Azure Heights? They get their souls eaten? We brought a daemon back, too. He's dead, but we can see him.

We know what they look like—these creatures that have been taking your people. Do *you* know what they look like?"

I had to give the guy credit. He kept his emotions under control. Because I couldn't read Maras like I could other creatures, I could only rely on body language to interpret their reactions. The faintest smile, flared nostrils, a fleeting sideways glance, or tightening shoulders—anything that could betray them. But the Correction Officers were cool, calm, and composed, like marble statues. They let nothing show.

I scoffed and ran up to the top level in what must have been record time. The Five Lords' mansions were guarded by Correction Officers, but the terrace was dark and quiet. The night had settled peacefully over the sumptuous estates, and droplets of fresh dew were forming on the petals of the crimson flowers adorning the front yards. Only the murmur of water from the central fountain could be heard, along with the occasional whisper of eastern winds.

"They're all comfy and snug in there," I muttered, feeding off my irritation as I anticipated seeing Caspian again, so soon after I'd learned he was our masked savior.

I stalked up to the Roho mansion first, and the Correction Officers moved to greet me.

"The Lords are resting," one of them said. "Come back in the morning."

"This can't wait," I replied bluntly. "Wake them up and get them out here, now. It's an emergency."

"Define 'emergency'," the other Mara said.

"An emergency is something that requires their immediate attention, unless you want to end up in the prison below as daemon chow for interfering with our investigation. Last time I checked your laws, obstruction of justice was a punishable offense."

They didn't react, except for a single muscle twitch in the first Mara's jaw. He nodded, then went to the Rohos' front door and knocked. I did the same with the other four mansions, then positioned myself by the fountain. I watched the lights flicker on inside, and waited for the Five Lords to come out.

As the minutes went by, I felt my nerves stretching, my mind bouncing between Fiona, the prison, and the massive daemon in the infirmary. Rowan was the first to come out, then Darius, Farrah, Emilian, and Caspian. None looked happy to see me, but I didn't exactly care. Scratch that. I didn't give a damn.

They walked over to the fountain, and I listened to the sound of water trickling behind me. It helped me stay focused and calm, since my heartrate decided to spike as soon as Caspian came into view. I straightened my back and proceeded to analyze the Exiled Maras' faces, trying to read them as best I could.

"This couldn't wait until the morning?" Farrah raised an eyebrow, while Caspian gave me his usual bone-chilling glare.

"One of our own was taken by a daemon," I said, and immediately took note of their expressions. Darius and Emilian frowned, Farrah seemed genuinely disconcerted, and Rowan brought a hand up to her mouth. "Fiona."

"Oh, no," Rowan gasped, then instinctively glanced over her shoulder, as if looking for Vincent. We all knew he had a thing for Fiona. We'd seen them dancing together, laughing and talking, at the Spring Ball. I figured Rowan was demonstrating motherly empathy, most likely trying to figure out a way to tell him.

"When did it happen?" Emilian's voice was low and gruff, and I sensed a slight tremor in it, too. Caspian remained quiet, his jade eyes fixed on me.

"Tonight," I replied. "She found your prison, down below. Daemons got in. They took her, but we have one of them."

"What do you mean, you have one of them?" Darius's brow furrowed.

"We killed and captured a daemon. It's why I'm here," I said. "I need you to come down to the infirmary with me. We will brief you on the specifics there."

Without another word, I turned around and headed downstairs. The Lords were completely silent as they followed. I heard additional footsteps behind us—Correction Officers staying close, their swords jingling in their metallic sheaths.

We reached the infirmary and went inside, where my team waited, standing next to the dead daemon.

"Oh, dear," Farrah gasped, her already-pale face turning stark white at the sight of the creature on the table.

The daemon was quite a sight, indeed—a powerful male specimen, with muscles galore and smooth, tanned skin. His sharp claws were extended, his horns were curved and pointy, and his fangs pressed against his lower lip. Patrik had fiddled with his joints and gums to better understand how they worked, and had left the claws and fangs out in full view for the Lords. The daemon's torso had been mangled by Blaze's dragon jaw, and blood had trickled down and pooled on the floor.

"Is... Is that it?" Emilian said, his voice barely audible as he came closer.

"This is one of them, yes," Jax replied, his hands resting on the handles of his swords, which hung loosely from his leather belt.

"This is a... daemon," Darius mumbled. "This is what has been taking our people?"

I analyzed their reactions carefully. They all seemed genuinely shocked. Rowan even seemed frightened by the creature lying on the table. Caspian, on the other hand, didn't even flinch, quietly confirming what I'd already suspected. He'd seen them before. He knew what they were, which made me wonder if the other Lords also knew, and were just really good at faking alarm.

"You look surprised." Jax scoffed. "I would've thought you knew what they looked like."

All five Maras' heads shot up, staring at him.

"Why would you say that?" Emilian asked.

"I've never seen one of these... things in my life!" Darius said, outrage blaring from his voice. "Why would you think we knew what they looked like?"

"I don't know." Jax shrugged. "Maybe because they were let loose inside *your* prison?"

"What are you talking about, Jaxxon?" Emilian was getting furious, his moustache twitching.

Hansa moved closer to Jax's side and crossed her arms over her chest.

"I was with Fiona down on the east side of the mountain wall, to bury a charm bag for the Druid's protection spell," Hansa explained. "We found a small, secluded beach down there, with an abandoned jetty and three massive tunnels. Someone wanted Fiona and me separated. I got conked on the head, and when I came to, the tunnel in the middle had collapsed and Fiona was nowhere to be found. I never saw who attacked me."

"We went down through the tunnel, after we cleared it," Caia continued. "The middle one leads straight into the prison, and, by the looks of what we saw inside, so do the other two on that eastern side of the mountain. We saw the cages. We saw Correction Officers guarding the place. We saw the gates come down. Fiona had made it in there, and she'd been looking around, trying to speak to your inmates."

I watched quietly as the Lords' expressions turned from shocked and confused to stern and dark. They were going into defensive mode as Blaze and Caia explained what they had seen down there, though Caspian was still made of stone, his gaze occasionally meeting mine. My frustration levels were spiking, mainly because he was the only one I had difficulty reading.

"The prisoners were all weak and delirious, barely able to speak," Blaze added. "Then a gong rang, and all the gates came down on the tunnel, so we couldn't get out. We heard one of your officers announce midnight, then one of the western gates went up. In their defense, the Correction Officers did sound surprised and seemed as though they wanted to bring it back down, but it was too late. Daemons came through. We couldn't tell you how many, since they were invisible. But they rushed into the prison, while the Correction Officers went into hiding. We fought the daemons off as best as we could, but one of them snatched Fiona."

"Most importantly, the daemons knew exactly what they were doing in there," Caia said. "They opened the prisoners' cages, and... How do I say this... Fed on their *souls*. I-I could *see* their souls, these little wisps of white energy, getting sucked out."

"I managed to kill one and bring it up here," Blaze concluded, nodding at the daemon on the table.

"So, please, Emilian, do tell us what is going on here, because clearly you've been holding back on us," Hansa said, her lips pressed into a thin line.

Emilian ran a hand through his hair before letting out an exasperated sigh. He then opened the infirmary door, summoning one of the Correction Officers.

"Get me the prison warden, now!" he barked, then shifted his focus back to us as the Correction Officer left the infirmary. "Hansa, believe me, we don't know anything about the daemons, nor the gates opening and closing in the prison. As for the prison itself, I assure you that it's all operated as per our legal standards. People who commit crimes go to jail. It's fairly simple."

"Then explain the state of your prisoners, all weak and pale and barely able to speak!" Jax shot back.

"The psyche of an inmate is beyond our concern." Caspian finally spoke up. "They're well fed and left to their own devices in those cages, but they are still prisoners. They are paying for their crimes. Do not question the legality of our measures; it really doesn't concern you. As for the gong you heard down there, it rings every six hours. It is the only notion of time passing that the inmates have."

"What about the gates?" I asked, raising an eyebrow and biting the inside of my cheek to stop myself from asking the burning questions that would surely bring him forward as our masked savior. I'd yet to decide whether he was being truthful regarding the lives that depended on his (and now my) secrecy.

"The gates," he said, glowering at me as if I'd insulted his mother's cooking, "are meant to stay down at all times, unless there is an emergency evacuation. Otherwise, no one should be able to get in from the outside. I do not know what happened with the eastern tunnels. I do not know who attacked Hansa."

He then turned to face Patrik, who stood next to Scarlett, Avril, and Heron by the map table.

"So, your protection spell clearly didn't work," Caspian added.

"It didn't because it didn't cover the prison," Patrik replied, his brow furrowed. He straightened his back, adopting a defensive attitude. There was a hint of regret in his voice, but he clearly didn't blame himself or his spell, given the Exiled Maras' secrecy. "It's underground, and we knew nothing about the tunnels. The daemons most likely snuck through them and made their way up to the second level tonight, bypassing the spell's perimeter. Had you told us about the prison and, most importantly, about the secret passages, I would've planned for a different area over which to cast the spell."

I felt the corner of my mouth twitch as I watched that exchange. It was mildly satisfying to watch the Lords get owned because of their own secrecy as they tried to blame our skills and magic for the daemons' presence. It had back-fired spectacularly.

"We'll probably have to seal the tunnels now, anyway, given how useful the daemons found them," Darius muttered, his gaze darting between Emilian, Caspian, Farrah, and Rowan, before it switched back to the daemon. "That thing is... ghastly..."

"How come we can see it now?" Farrah asked, inching closer to the creature.

"We don't know how they make themselves invisible," Patrik replied. "I'll have to do some further analysis, but we do know how to make them visible. Water destroys whatever cloaking mechanism they employ."

Once again, Caspian didn't react, while the other Lords' eyebrows rose. I could feel my eyes shrinking to slits. I couldn't help but further suspect Caspian of knowing way more about the daemons than he was letting on. My fists weighed heavily at my sides, my nails digging into my palms as I bit my lower lip, trying to figure out the enigma that was Caspian Kifo.

2

AVRIL

(DAUGHTER OF LUCAS & MARION)

The infirmary door swung open, and two Correction Officers pushed the prison warden into the room before resuming their positions outside. The warden, an Exiled Mara with short gray-speckled hair and pale blue eyes, looked downright terrified as he stood before us.

A clock was ticking in my mind. Time slipped by, and I needed to be out there, with my team, rescuing Fiona. I could feel my patience wearing thin. Fortunately, the Lords seemed to be on the same page as me.

"What happened down there? What happened to the gates?" Caspian's voice was low and cold, seemingly frightening the old warden. Lord Kifo shortened the distance between them in just two lightning-fast steps, and grabbed him by his shirt collar. "What. Happened. Down. There?"

"My... My apologies, milord," the warden squealed. "We'd had technical issues with those gates all day... I don't know exactly what happened, but I thought the problem had been fixed. They changed some gears and oiled them properly, and we left the gates up until midnight so the oils could slip all the way through the mechanisms."

"Did you have guards stationed at the end of each tunnel while the gates were up?" Caspian asked, a vein throbbing in his temple. He was angry, and deservedly so. Though I'd yet to clear the Lords of any suspicion, their outrage had come across as genuine. They seemed protective of their legal system, sure, but nothing pointed specifically to them knowing about the daemons, especially based on what the warden was telling us.

"No, milord." The warden shook his head.

"Why not?"

"I... I didn't see the need, given how packed with Correction Officers the prison itself is, milord... It was a mistake."

"And the western gate that went up?" Caspian replied, briefly looking at Blaze and Caia.

"I swear, milord, we still don't know what happened there." The warden shuddered under his grip. "It was meant to stay down. The mechanisms are automatic and linked to the levers. We don't know how that gate went up, but none of our Correction Officers did it... I swear, milord."

"Did you see them?" Caia frowned. The warden looked at her with mild confusion. "The daemons. Did you see them come in and crack open cage doors and feed on your prisoners' souls?"

"Not really, no... I wasn't down there at the time. I was in my office. One of the guards came up and told me what had happened, told me there were strange, invisible entities below. The Correction Officers left the prison once your dragon got loose!"

"But the western gate went back down shortly afterward," Blaze growled. "Was that another glitch? Having the daemons go in for dinner, then bringing the gate down right after they leave?"

"No, one of our mechanics managed to fix it from above!" the warden replied.

Several moments passed in heavy silence before Jax exhaled, then rested his hands on his hips and scowled at the Lords.

"I swear, these unpleasant coincidences keep stacking up against you," he said, shaking his head.

"Don't be melodramatic," Darius shot back. "Those daemons were most likely prowling the western tunnels. They must have discovered them from the plain. The gate malfunction would have been a gift from the heavens for them, since there are plenty of defenseless inmates down there. It's bad enough we failed our own people by endangering the lives of these prisoners—who, despite being criminals, are still citizens of Azure Heights. We don't need you to chastise us and accuse us of... what, exactly?"

"There's an ongoing list right now," Jax muttered, "but it's too early to lay it out for you."

"What my colleague is trying to say," Hansa intervened, giving him a sideways glance, "is that you haven't been exactly forthcoming over the past couple of days, and it has cost us one of our own. It would have also cost you more of *your* people, including Rewa, had it not been for us patrolling the second level tonight."

At the sound of his daughter's name, Darius's face went blank.

"What... What do you mean?" he gasped.

"You weren't aware? I'm surprised she didn't tell you." Hansa raised an eyebrow. "She was on the second level tonight with two of her servants. They were attacked by daemons, and we saved them. They sought refuge in the tavern above. The nurses went up there, treated their wounds with Mara blood, then sent them home. Have you not seen Rewa tonight?"

Darius nearly lost his balance as Hansa's words crashed into him. During our brief study of the dead daemon, one of the nurses had poked her head in and told us about the girls having been sent home. Their wounds had been shallow, despite the bleeding, and were quickly healed. Come to think of it, the Lords should have already been down here after we'd rescued Rewa and she'd returned home...

"I haven't seen Rewa since dinner," Darius mumbled. "I had a serious argument with her about going out at such late hours. I'd specifically prohibited such escapades... Rewa probably went against my word and didn't tell me because she was afraid I'd punish her."

"Parenting 101." Harper scoffed. "Tell your kid she can't do something, and that's exactly what she'll do. Nice to see the Mara parents have it just as hard as ours."

Darius shook his head, ignoring Harper's remark, then opened the infirmary door and called out to one of the Correction Officers.

"Take this incompetent fool to holding," he said, pointing at the warden. "I trust Lord Kifo will appoint someone else to take his place in the morning. And go check on my daughter, make sure she's in her room and doesn't leave the house. I want a protective detail on her from now on. Have her wait for me there. I'll need a word with her."

The Correction Officer did as instructed and took the warden out of the infirmary, while Darius closed the door and turned to face us again.

"Can you redo the protection spell?" he asked, glancing at Patrik. "To cover the tunnels and prison, this time?"

"I need access to a north, south, west, and east tunnel to do that," the Druid replied, "but yes, I can do it again, to avoid another infiltration like tonight. I still can't guarantee it will work against them, given that we know very little about the daemons."

"Good. It's better than nothing. I'll have Correction Officers escort you, for your safety," Caspian said. "We'll have to investigate the tunnels and seal them all for the time being, anyway, given that the daemons are now coming through them and bypassing the edges of your protection spell."

"Yeah, we're not doing anything before we get Fiona back," Jax shot back. "You can get started on sealing your tunnels, for now. We need to go find our agent."

"How can we help?" Emilian asked.

"Glad you asked." Harper smirked. "Our whole team is going this time. We need fifty to seventy Correction Officers with us, for backup."

"Excuse me?" Caspian blurted. "I'm not going to risk that many of my officers for this. It's suicide. You've been to the Valley of Screams. You've seen what's in there!"

"First of all, no, you're not excused," Harper replied calmly. "Second, we now know what the daemons look like and how to disrupt their invisibility; therefore, we have an advantage we didn't have when we first went in there. Third, we are not losing Fiona to that place, and we need your help. After the prison gate debacle, it is *literally* the least you can do. And, last but not least, I honestly think it's in *your* best interest to work with us on this."

Caspian's forehead smoothed and his nostrils flared. She'd managed to get to him, and I couldn't help but wonder what Harper had meant by emphasizing *his* best interest. I'd have to ask her about it later, though. For now, the focus had shifted back to Fiona, and we needed to get moving.

"Fine," Caspian said, gritting his teeth. "I'll have fifty of my best Maras ready within the hour."

"Thank you, Lord Kifo." Harper's half-smile echoed a tremendous amount of satisfaction, which was short-lived, as Caspian sneered at her.

"Would you mind if we have a word? In private?" he asked.

Harper stilled, then looked at Hansa and Jax. They both frowned but eventually nodded. Harper sighed and walked out of the infirmary, followed by Caspian. Jax then clapped his hands once, commanding our full attention.

"GASP team, go get all your war gear and shields," he instructed. "Anything that can help against the daemons, bring it with you. We leave within the hour, as soon as Lord Kifo's Correction Officers are ready."

"I'll have my servants bring down our strongest indigo horses for your team," Emilian said. "You need speed and endurance in those gorges."

"Thank you, Lord Obara." Jax gave him a polite nod. "It's much appreciated."

"It is the least we can do, as you say," Emilian replied, then gave Hansa a weak smile. "I know we have our differences, but we sincerely wish to support you in your quest to rid us of this daemon menace."

I was the first to leave and head for the inn, followed

closely by Heron, Blaze, Caia, Scarlett, and Patrik. Jax and Hansa decided to stay behind, and gave Heron and me instructions on what weapons and gear to bring back for them.

The night was cool and eerily quiet, except for the occasional scream echoing from the gorges. I cringed as we raced up the stairs, praying to all the divine entities out there that none of those wails belonged to Fiona.

Hold on, babe, we're coming.

3

HARPER

(DAUGHTER OF HAZEL & TEJUS)

As soon as I stepped outside the infirmary, Caspian's hand firmly clasped mine and pulled me around the corner, down a side alley. He constantly looked around and over his shoulder.

"Where are we going?" I asked, but he shushed me, his fingers digging into my skin. His touch sent millions of tiny electrical impulses through my body, but I didn't want to focus on the effect he had on me. I was too worried about Fiona to allow myself the luxury of enjoying his touch.

Wait, enjoying *his touch? Why am I even—*

Before I could finish chastising myself, he turned left into a dark and narrow street, then came to a sudden halt. He bent down and pulled open a trapdoor neatly covered in slim cobblestones to imitate the rest of the road. I hadn't even seen it.

He slipped inside, lowering himself onto a wooden ladder, then glanced up and waited for me to follow.

"What's this?" I asked, and he shushed me again.

Judging by the irritated look on his face, he needed me down there before he could speak.

What in the world is he up to?

I rolled my eyes, then climbed down the short ladder. He pulled the trapdoor shut, then turned to face me. A couple of seconds went by as his jade gaze pierced through me, setting my cheeks on fire for no apparent reason. I hated the way my body reacted to his mere presence. It threw me off my game.

"Okay, what is this?" I asked again, motioning around at the small chamber he'd brought us to. Its walls, floor, and ceiling were paneled with wood, and I could see another trapdoor in a corner, despite the darkness.

"It's a sealed bunker. I have dozens of these throughout the city," he replied, then pointed at the floor. "That leads into a small tunnel. Each bunker has one. They're secret routes through, as well as in and out of, the city. The bunkers and the tunnels are all coated in meranium."

"Am I supposed to know what that is?"

"It's a Nerakian metal. All our blades are made from it. It's strong and doesn't oxidize and, most importantly, has some special properties," he explained. "Soundproofing is one of them. No one can hear us talk in here."

"So no one can hear me scream in here," I muttered, crossing my arms over my chest.

He raised an eyebrow and pursed his lips in response. I'd obviously insulted him, but I was enjoying it a little too much to feel sorry.

"I have more than one way of making you scream, Miss Hellswan. You'll have to be more specific."

Caspian's voice dropped by a couple of degrees, reaching freezing temperatures as he watched my eyes widen—a reaction I couldn't control.

"Then you wonder why I find it hard to trust you," I shot back, then shook my head to regain some of the focus I'd just lost. "What's up with the tunnels?"

"They had nothing to do with the daemons getting onto the second level," he replied. "Meranium is the one metal I know they're extremely allergic to. Plus, the tunnels are too small to fit them. They're mostly used by Imen."

"And what do the Imen do with these tunnels, then?"

"I'll tell you about it later." He brushed me off with the wave of a hand, as if my question were completely irrelevant. It further contributed to my frustration, but I needed to keep my cool and find another way to figure him out. Getting on his bad side was not going to help. "It really isn't important now, and it has nothing to do with why I brought you here."

I took a deep breath and rubbed my face with my palms. It had been a long night already, and it was starting to feel interminable.

"*Why* am I here, Caspian?"

He scoffed, breathing heavily as he took a step forward, getting closer. I feared he'd hear my heart suddenly beating faster, so I cleared my throat, as if hoping it would cover the frantic thuds in my chest.

"What the hell were you thinking up there?" he hissed. "Blackmailing me? Really? You're asking me to send fifty of my Maras to die with you in the Valley of Screams!"

"I'll do whatever it takes to get Fiona back." I held my chin up, firm and unyielding. I had every intention of making sure we came out of this alive and in one piece. Having a dragon on our side greatly increased our chances. However, even though we could leave the scorching daemons part to Blaze, we needed manpower to cover all angles. The Exiled Maras were trained to guard and attack, and had better knowledge of those gorges. It wasn't a light decision to make by any means, but we needed Caspian's people with us for backup. Fiona's life was worth it—we'd come here to help them, and, had they been more forthcoming about those damn tunnels and the prison in the first place, we wouldn't be in this mess.

"Didn't you hear what I just said? My Correction Officers will most likely *die* protecting your stubborn asses! I'm sorry about your friend, but why don't you be a smart vampire and cut your losses? Leave Neraka now, before you all get killed in those gorges. There's no point in dragging my people down with you."

"You need to get something through your thick head, because I obviously haven't made myself clear enough," I shot back, my blood boiling. I poked him in the chest with my index finger—a habit I seemed to have developed when arguing with Caspian. "I will stop at nothing to get Fiona back. I need your Correction Officers for backup while I turn those gorges upside down and wash them in dragon fire! I will kill every daemon I come across until I find Fiona and get her back safe! You either help me, or I tell your fellow Lords that you were the one who helped us in the Valley of Screams. Your choice! Either way, we are going down there tonight. And I genuinely feel sorry for anyone standing in our way. Blaze is really fired up tonight, and I can't wait to watch him burn it all down!"

Caspian stared at me, his gaze softening for a split second, before the jade in his eyes turned stone cold again and he let out a frustrated sigh.

"Clearly, there's no way for me to talk sense into you," he said bitterly. "You don't understand what these creatures are capable of. You'll die there, Miss Hellswan."

"Maybe." I shrugged, then gave him a wink. "But I'm not that easy to kill. If anything, you could tell me more about the daemons and your involvement in this whole mess, so I

can at least do a better job of keeping your Correction Officers alive down there."

"Trust me, Miss Hellswan, you don't want to know."

I couldn't help but like the way my name sounded
rolling off his tongue, despite the dark context.

Get a grip!

"Actually, I obviously do, but if you refuse to share more,
we'll have to make do," I replied. "We're going to get Fiona
back. If you won't tell me more, at least help me."

"I'll help you get torn to shreds, sure." He shook his
head, then pulled out a handful of disc-shaped medallions
from his waistcoat pocket. "Put your hand out."

I did as he asked, and he placed the metallic discs in my
palm. They were small but sturdy, complete with thin
chains. I stared at them, counting ten medallions.

"What are these?" I asked.

"There's one for each GASP member, including Fiona.
Provided, of course, that you find her alive," Caspian
replied. "They're made of meranium, both pendant and
chain. The daemons won't be able to stay close to you for
too long. It won't stop them from trying to kill you, but
there's enough meranium in these things to keep them from
consuming your souls."

"So you knew about the soul-eating part." I glowered at
him. "Damn it, Caspian, you could've said something
earlier, if you really wanted to help!"

"Who said I want to help?" His question cut through me, and a possible truth started to sink in.

"Then why *did* you help us? Back in the Valley of Screams... and tonight, as well. And now, with these pendants. If you don't want to help, *why* are you helping us? It doesn't make sense."

Every second I spent near him dazed me further, to the point where I had trouble using basic logic. But everything Caspian had done so far had been contradictory. On one hand, he wanted us off the planet. On the other, he'd swooped in, and gotten himself injured in the process, just to help us fight off the daemons. With no clear understanding of his intentions, I was at a loss.

I stared at him, wishing so much that I could read his emotions, see ribbons of color coming out of him, so I could understand what he was thinking. He lowered his head, inching closer to my face. I craned my neck back a little to maintain eye contact. My stomach tightened.

"I wish I had an answer to that, Miss Hellswan, but I don't," he replied, his tone softer despite his marble expression.

"Well... thanks for these," I mumbled, and looked down at the pendants, unable to hold his gaze without feeling my blood rush through my limbs in waves of hot and cold.

"Don't thank me," he said, his gaze darkening. "I'm only trying to give you all a quick death. Dying from soul consumption is something I wouldn't wish upon my worst enemy, and it's something I'm trying to stop from happening to my people, which is why I'm compelled to kindly ask you again that you keep my identity secret. No one in this city can know what I did for you."

"Well, according to you, we're off to our deaths, anyway, so I wouldn't worry too much about me telling on you," I replied. "But if we do make it back alive, I *will* have questions for you. Lots of them."

He gave me a weak smile, and my heart skipped a beat. He looked... genuinely sad for a second.

"I'm sure you will," he whispered, and I could swear I caught a hint of grief in his faded voice. "Goodbye, Miss Hellswan."

He moved past me, his shoulder brushing against mine as he climbed up the ladder and pushed the trapdoor open. I followed quietly, feeling a chill sneak into my ribcage and clutch my heart. Its grip was tight and icy, and it was an emotion I'd rarely had the misfortune to experience. It was dread, and it came from the way in which Caspian had said goodbye. It sounded final.

I watched as he closed the trapdoor behind us and walked away down the street, vanishing around a corner without even bothering to cast me one last glance.

I slipped one of the pendants around my neck, hiding it beneath my leather suit, then shoved the others in my pocket. I had to get these back to my team, and I had to explain how I got them, and what they did, without any Exiled Maras overhearing us.

"I'll need a piece of paper," I muttered, shoving any last thoughts of Caspian aside and heading back to the infirmary.

4

FIONA

(DAUGHTER OF BENEDICT & YELENA)

My head hurt, like dozens of hammers were pummeling my brain from different angles. I heard water dripping somewhere nearby, and it echoed around me. Other than that, all was silent. I groaned, then peeled my eyes open. They adjusted slowly to the dim light. I reached out, and my hand found a succession of iron bars.

Where am I?

Memories of the previous hours crashed into me. The small beach. The tunnel. The prison and its gates opening and closing. The daemons coming to feed on the inmates' souls.

I was taken...

I gasped and instantly sat up, dread washing over me in icy waves as I briefly analyzed my surroundings. I was in a cage made entirely out of solid black iron. Said cage was inside a large grotto, its walls pale pink, with a myriad of crystal formations overhead. Orange flames flickered from a fire on the stone floor, and the light shimmered against the crystals, summoning shades of pink, amethyst, and yellow to spread through the cave.

There was a small pond not far from the fire. It had been carved into the floor—whether by hand or by nature, I wasn't sure, but its water was a beautiful sapphire blue, and steam rolled out of it. It was some kind of thermal water, with bubbles occasionally rising up. Despite my grim circumstances, I couldn't help but marvel at the natural beauty around me.

The air rippled subtly in the corner to my left, and I froze, my nerves stretching and my muscles turning into hard stone as I realized the daemon that had taken me was still here with me. I remembered being held tight, unable to break free despite my supernatural strength, as the daemon carried me out onto the plain. Then yellow dust had been blown in my face and everything had gone dark.

It drugged me...

It was more sophisticated than I'd initially thought. It used powders to stun its victims. It held its prey in cages hidden deep inside the gorges.

It consumed *souls*.

This was no ordinary hostile, and I couldn't even see what it looked like. My heart thumped loudly. I understood that my only chance of survival was to get myself out of the cage. I pulled on the bars and felt the metal slowly give, creaking under my grip.

My pulse raced as the air rippled closer. A puff of red dust blew in my face. I fell back, landing on my elbows, wheezing and coughing. My arms and legs tingled while I struggled to sit back up, but I was suddenly too weak, as if my muscles had turned to jelly. I managed to pull myself to one side of the cage, still facing the invisible daemon, and lean against the bars.

"What did you do to me?" I asked, not sure I'd get an answer.

My entire body was ridiculously relaxed, and I didn't have the strength to pull those iron bars apart anymore. Whatever that red powder was, it had done a number on my muscles and significantly reduced my strength.

"Who are you? What are you? Why am I here?"

It didn't respond, but I could sense it standing close to my cage. I caught glimpses of its glowing red eyes as it leaned forward, staring at me. I felt its hot breath on my face, but I did my best to stay calm. If it wanted me dead, all it had to do was pull me out of the cage.

I remembered the knives I'd hidden in my boots before going out to the eastern mountain wall. I patted my hips and couldn't find my swords, or even my belt with its many useful satchels. I then reached down to my boot, feeling for the knife handle, but there was nothing there. I held my breath, realizing that the creature had completely disarmed me.

My blood clotted in thick ice clusters as I watched one of my knives lift off the floor in front of me and into the air, wielded by the invisible daemon. It was holding it by the tip of its blade, showing it to me. The knife then fell to the ground with a sharp clang, next to my other weapons and my belt, and I suddenly felt anger animating my blood vessels and jumpstarting my heart. The daemon was mocking me.

"Aw, good for you, you got my weapons," I sneered. "My teammates are on their way to get me. They'll turn these gorges upside down. They'll burn you alive, and you won't stand a chance, invisible or otherwise!"

It huffed at me, but I wasn't sure whether it was out of amusement or contempt. Nevertheless, it was a reaction. Which meant that it understood me.

"You daemons really don't know what you're getting yourselves into," I continued. "You should've stayed in these gorges, but you got greedy, and you won't like what's coming next. In case you didn't notice it back in the prison, we have a freakin' dragon!"

I didn't get a reaction this time, but I caught movement as the daemon seemed to leave the cave through a small tunnel twenty feet to my left. I looked around, trying to analyze every detail and see if there was anything in the grotto that I could use to set myself free. There was nothing within my reach, just a bunch of furs piled up by the fire, and my weapons and belt too far for me to reach.

I'm not getting eaten in this place...

A squeal outside caught my attention.

I need to find a way out.

The sound of an animal being dragged inside made me still. I watched as the invisible daemon brought in a dead creature resembling a wild boar. My hands instinctively covered my mouth as it peeled the skin off the boar, slicing chunks of flesh off and swallowing them whole. I then watched it take one piece of meat and hold it over the fire for a couple of minutes, enough to roast it a little.

I slid to the back of my cage as it brought the piece of meat close, slipping it between the iron bars and dropping it in my lap. I'd been under the impression that my cage was big enough to stay out of reach, but clearly its arm was longer than I'd imagined... assuming it did have arms. I was speechless.

Is it... Is it trying to... feed me?

"Is this for me?" I mumbled, holding the chunk of meat between my thumb and index finger. I looked in the daemon's red eyes before they vanished for a second, then reappeared. I took a deep breath and thought of ways to get myself out of there, one way or another. Perhaps befriending the fiend might work. "I'm sorry, but I don't eat meat. I don't eat anything. I only drink blood."

I put the meat down on the ground and watched as it

was removed from my cage and tossed into the fire. I had a feeling it didn't eat cooked meat, only raw flesh. I moved closer to the bars, enough to feel its hot breath touching my face again.

"I'm not a Mara, if that's what you're thinking," I said, and its eyes flickered a peculiar bright red before disappearing again. I couldn't wrap my head around how its invisibility worked. "I'm a vampire. Not from around here. I have fangs and pale skin, and I drink blood and don't do sunlight, just like the Maras. In a broad sense, we belong to the same subset of species. But I'm different. I was made a vampire, rather than born one."

It stood there for a while, in silence. I tried to listen in on its breathing or heartbeat, but it didn't give anything away. It sniffed me; then I felt its touch on my cheek. I was unable to move as its skin met mine. Warmth spread through my face, lighting my temples on fire before the daemon pulled away and rushed back outside.

I heard another squeal a minute or two later and found myself gaping as it dragged in another wild boar—this one very much alive and kicking, squealing and struggling to escape the daemon's hold.

Tough luck, buddy. I tried that too... Didn't work out too well for me.

The daemon slit the animal's throat, and I yelped, then covered my mouth with one hand. This creature was taking me on an emotional rollercoaster ride, and I had a hard time keeping up. It pushed the dead boar's head between the iron bars, enough for its open wound to gush into my cage. The blood poured in a thin, steady stream.

It hit me then what the daemon wanted me to do. And I didn't think I could say no, not unless I wanted to piss it off.

I needed my captor calm and pleased, and I hadn't drunk any blood since early morning, so I cupped my hands beneath the boar's open throat and drank a pint's worth of blood. The daemon then tossed the animal aside, while I swallowed the last of my unexpected meal. I wiped my mouth with the back of my hand, then took a deep breath. The creature stood before me, its red eyes drilling into me.

"Thank you," I murmured. "That was very kind of you."

It got closer again, prompting me to hold my breath. I felt its fingers—I guessed—on my cheek, gently sliding down and over my lower lip. I noticed the blood droplet it collected, then watched it disappear into what had to be its mouth, since it was briefly followed by a short suckling sound. My stomach tightened, and I didn't know how to react, but my cheeks were quite adept at catching fire in the creature's presence. That made me uncomfortable.

"You are one demented weirdo, you know that?" I said, forgetting to dial back the sass. After all, he'd only just fed me. "You should really let me go before my team finds us here. You'll have a chance to survive. It's the best I can do, given the circumstances—let me out now, and I won't bring them here. I will keep them away. I promise."

I heard it snicker then—a low, guttural growl, actually, that sounded both amused and insulted. It huffed once more, then darted over to the pond and jumped in with a messy splash. Water spilled over the sharp edges as it dove deeper. I couldn't take my eyes off it.

A dark figure appeared beneath the turquoise water. It then emerged in all its visible glory, and my chest burned, my mind expanded, and my lungs stopped functioning altogether.

It was a "he".

A massive, stunning man, much taller than Heron or Jax, probably by at least two heads. His shoulders were broad, his hips beautifully sculpted, their curved lines disappearing beneath a chainmail loincloth hung loosely from a thin leather belt. Horns emerged from the back of his head and grew forward, pointed and smooth. His hair was long, a rich black that fell down his back, and his eyes were glowing red. His face was a sculptural masterpiece with a stern jaw, high cheekbones, and a straight nose.

My heart started racing as I suddenly remembered that I needed it to work in order to breathe and continue gaping at the now-visible daemon. Ropes of muscle covered every inch of his body, big enough to make him look menacing, but toned and sculpted to maybe honor ancient Greek statues of athletes. His skin was a deep shade of tan, luscious and wet, and droplets of water rolled down his shoulders and abs.

He sauntered back to my cage with a smirk that made me blink several times.

He was *nothing* like what I'd expected.

Black tattoos covered his chest and arms, sequences of geometric symbols and perfectly circular swirls beaten into his skin. I guessed they had to mean something. Aside from the humans on Earth, who mostly got tattoos just for aesthetic purposes, all the other creatures I'd met marked their skin for specific reasons—social status, tribal indication, or mystical abilities. I wondered what the daemon's tattoos signified.

He drew closer, his face now inches from mine, yet I remained rooted to the spot, unable to back away. He looked at me intently, giving me enough time to study his eyes. They were a deep ruby red with a thin black border and flakes of gold, shadowed by long eyelashes and elegant brows.

I was stunned speechless.

He reached out abruptly and clasped my chin, causing my breath to hitch in surprise. He then pushed it up, closing my mouth. A flicker of amusement passed over his face. I realized that I'd been literally gawking at him, my mandible dislodged from the rest of my head.

Say something. Do something. Come on, Fiona...

I couldn't. The daemon cocked his head to one side, his gaze searing through me like hot lava, his lips full and tender as they stretched into a most arrogant grin.

"You should be more worried about yourself right now. Your team is as good as dead," he spoke up, and I heard his voice for the first time, rumbling through me like thunder.

It was calm, low, and husky, exuding self-confidence and the kind of determination that made me understand that I had my hands full with this guy.

I really need to get out of here.

5

SCARLETT

(DAUGHTER OF JERAMIAH & PIPPA)

W e geared up and met inside the infirmary half an hour later. I carried my long sword, along with two large knives on my belt and smaller blades tucked in my boots. My backpack was filled with prepped swamp witch spells and fist-sized explosive balls I'd devised from a combination of gunpowder and dragon tears.

The map of the gorges was laid out on the table, and we all looked over it. The rest of our team was equally loaded with weapons and enough tension to probably blow up the Valley of Screams. The air was thick between us, charged with anger and determination.

"This is, by far, the best route we can take." Avril pointed at the map, her finger following a sinuous line along a stream. "The water will come in handy to counter the invisibility aspect of the daemons, and it holds the most caves. The Exiled Maras know about most of those, anyway."

"This is where we found Minah, more or less." Jax's finger moved to a neighboring gorge, then back to the stream. "And this is where we found Darius after the attack. So, up to this point, we have a pretty good idea as to what's in that gorge. What lies beyond, however, is foreign to us. I need you to be on your toes at all times. The Correction Officers will have our backs; it'll be our job to cover our sides and the front."

We all nodded, then Caia cleared her throat.

"Once we get Fiona back," she said, "one of us will go back to Calliope and rally more agents, like we agreed."

"Yes, Caia, but it won't be you," Hansa replied. "You've got fire, and we need it here."

"Understood," she said, then frowned as she went over the interview notes. "What about Demios, Arrah's brother?"

"We'll have to sneak into the prison and look for him," Avril replied, crossing her arms over her chest. "I think we can use the invisibility spell supply that we have for this, right, Jax?"

Jax thought about it for a second, then gave Patrik a sideways glance.

"What do you think, Druid? You're the one in charge of our magic supply inventory," he quipped.

"Perfectly doable," Patrik replied. "I can spare enough for one, even two of us, just for prison use."

"Good. Now that's out of the way, back to Fiona." Jax sighed, then peeked through the window, noticing the fifty Correction Officers gathering outside on their horses. "They're almost ready."

"Let's get moving, then," Hansa replied. "Our relationship with the Lords is fragile enough as it is—I don't want to keep their people waiting, too. It's bad enough we'll break into their prison soon. Pack the gorge map, please."

Avril rolled the map into a tube and shoved it into a leather satchel hanging from her shoulder as we all moved to the door.

"Wait," Harper said, scribbling a few lines on a piece of paper. "I have something for us."

She placed nine disc-shaped pendants on the table, and handed the written note to Hansa.

"What are those?" I asked, but Hansa immediately shushed me as she read Harper's message. She passed the paper on to Jax, who skimmed it, frowned, and gave it to Heron. The paper made its way from one member of our team to another, until it reached Patrik.

I craned my neck to get a better look, unaware of how close my face was getting to his until I felt warmth radiating from his cheek and his deep blue eyes quietly studying me. He handed me Harper's message, and I nodded my thanks, stepping back to read it.

No better way to say it, but I will explain later when we're all alone, I promise. Caspian is the masked guy who helped us in the gorges and on the second level. He knows more about the daemons than the others, but no one knows he helped us. He gave me these pendants for us to wear. They're made of meranium, a local metal, which stops the daemons from eating our souls. Won't completely protect us from them but will help. Put them on, keep it to yourselves, destroy this note. Walls might have ears.

"Well, then," Hansa said as she put one of the pendants around her neck, while we grabbed ours. "We clearly have a lot to talk over later."

"I need everyone out now," Patrik replied, while I borrowed one of Caia's lighters and burned the note.

He drew several chalk symbols on the walls and around the door and windows, while we left the infirmary and waited outside. He muttered a spell, then locked the door and joined us on the terrace, where the Correction Officers waited.

"I sealed the infirmary," he said, looking around. "It won't allow anyone in other than myself."

The Correction Officers were lined up on the main road leading to the plains below, patiently waiting for us. Patrik moved closer to my side, and his arm bumped my shoulder, prompting me to look at him. He gave me a reassuring nod. He'd probably noticed the frown I'd been wearing since Fiona had been taken, and was trying to make me feel better. He succeeded, if only by a degree or two, which was enough for me to give him a weak smile in return.

"We'll comb those gorges until we get her back, Scarlett," he said slowly. "I promise."

Imen servants came down with ten beautiful indigo horses, one of which was for Fiona. They were strong specimens with long black manes, leather saddles, and metallic plates molded onto their broad, muscular chests, for protection.

"We're using the tracking spell again, right?" Caia asked. I nodded and fumbled through my pockets until I found Fiona's bracelets, holding them up for her to see.

"I'll cast it soon," Patrik replied softly, sensing her anxiousness to get to Fiona.

We were all strained and eager to get our "iron fist" back, which was why we didn't even notice an eleventh indigo horse approaching, ridden by Vincent, of House Roho. I was surprised to see him wearing a combat uniform similar to the Correction Officers'—all black leather and metal plates, with plenty of bladed weapons and large, round shields. In place of their usual attire, the Maras had opted for a more military style, fit for the darkness and hostility that awaited in the Valley of Screams.

Their Nerakian horses huffed and neighed, clicking their hooves against the cobblestones and occasionally shaking their heads. I had a feeling the creatures were as nervous as we were.

6

HARPER

(DAUGHTER OF HAZEL & TEJUS)

Seeing Vincent all dressed up to go to war came as a surprise to all of us, but I was the first to point it out, while the Imen servants brought the indigo horses closer.

"Lord Roho, what are you doing here?" I asked as I was handed the reins to a gorgeous mare with deep midnight-blue eyes.

"I'm coming with you," he said, his chin high. A curved sword hung from his belt, tucked into a carved scabbard made of white bone and adorned with a variety of colored gems.

"I'm sorry, I thought I heard you say you were coming with us?" Hansa's sarcasm didn't escape any of us. Not even Vincent, who smirked and firmly gripped the handle of his sword.

"You heard right. I am coming with you," he replied.

"What makes you think we'll allow that?" Jax interjected as he climbed onto his horse, his tone dry and lacking patience.

"It's not like you can stop me." Vincent raised an eyebrow. "As soon as my mother told me about Fiona, I knew I had to be involved. I'm coming with you because I need to be a part of this. Fiona is important to me."

"Milord, you're clearly underestimating the dangers of this mission." Hansa scoffed, settling on her indigo mare. The creature seemed at ease with her new rider, her muscles twitching with anticipation.

"Maybe, but that won't stop me from going," Vincent replied. "I may not be a warrior such as yourselves, but I can surely hold my own in a fight. I did learn how to use a sword as a child."

"Yeah, that's not very reassuring," I said with a cringe. "We're not going into a bar fight armed with pig stickers. We're venturing into extremely hostile territory inhabited by bloodthirsty daemons with claws, horns, and fangs eager to rip you to shreds. Oh, and they're invisible, too."

"I thought you had the invisibility issue solved." Vincent grinned.

"Milord, that's not the issue here." Hansa pinched the bridge of her nose, trying to find the right words to explain Vincent's inadequacy as part of our detail. "You head the art department of the city. You deal with... design and beauty on a daily basis. You're not cut out for this. You don't have any training that would make you fit to come with us. If anything, we'd have to worry about your safety down there, along with our prime objective, and getting Fiona back alive and in one piece is all that matters. We cannot spare any resources to keep you safe just because you want some action. This isn't a game, milord."

"We've already seen Maras die during our first incursion into the Valley of Screams," Jax added, moving his horse closer to Hansa's. "And I doubt you'll make it out of there alive."

But Vincent wouldn't budge. He shook his head and clicked his teeth, prompting his horse to come forward.

"I'm not asking for your protection, nor am I holding you responsible for my safety and wellbeing," he replied. "Trust me, I can take care of myself, and I sincerely wish to help. I need to be there with you to find Fiona."

A couple of moments flew by as we all looked at each other. I didn't bother to hide my skepticism, keeping an eyebrow raised and my lips pursed, until Jax's shoulders dropped and he let out a frustrated groan.

"Fine, you can come with us," he muttered, and Vincent lit up like a Christmas tree. "I just hope you don't regret it."

"I won't," Vincent replied, nodding briefly. "And I promise I will not be a burden."

"In that case, Vincent," Caspian chimed in, emerging from behind a corner of the infirmary with his hands behind his back, "I'll let the Lords know that you've relinquished any need for protection from GASP *or* my Correction Officers."

"The Correction Officers shouldn't be excluded from this agreement," Vincent sneered. "I'm certainly not consenting to not at least have *them* nearby. Not that I'll need them, but still, just in case."

"Then you might want to get on my officers' good sides, Vincent, and do your best not to be the demanding little jerk you usually are," Caspian shot back, stifling a grin.

Vincent opened his mouth to respond, but was abruptly interrupted by Patrik, who cleared his throat loudly and brought out the round crystal pendant for Fiona's tracking spell.

"Time to get moving," Patrik announced as Scarlett handed him one of Fiona's bracelets.

He placed the pendant on top of the bracelet and chanted the spell, launching the bright luminescent sphere into the air. It didn't shoot out, but gently hovered above the Correction Officers before it moved slowly down the road.

"Isn't it supposed to go faster?" Caia asked.

"Not at this point," Patrik replied. "Its speed depends on proximity to its target. The farther Fiona is, the slower the tracking spell moves, as it registers the small traces that her body leaves behind."

"It's like a magical hound dog," I said, impressed by the

glowing light. "The stronger the scent, the faster the tracker, I suppose."

"Indeed. Based on what we know about the tunnels below, Caia and Blaze were much closer to Fiona earlier than we are now. The closer we get to her, the faster we'll have to go to keep up with the spell. In the meantime, however, we need to follow the light."

The analogy suddenly hit me, and I needed to let it out, noticing the gloomy expressions on Caia and Blaze's faces.

"Ugh, cheer up, guys," I quipped. "Think about it this way: you both followed that light to the end of a tunnel and came out alive. That's something!"

They both gave me their best versions of a smile, given the circumstances, and I knew I'd done the best I could to help improve their morale. We couldn't afford to go into those gorges with our heads down or doubt in our hearts.

We took our indigo horses down the main road, followed by Vincent and the fifty Correction Officers, as the tracking spell guided us toward the open field. I briefly glanced over my shoulder and saw Caspian watching us— me, in particular—as we descended the mountain. He stayed behind, his shoulder casually resting against a street lamp while our group moved forward, and I felt a spike of irritation at his laid-back demeanor.

For some reason, my blood always seemed to simmer when he was around. It felt like I'd become so much more intense as a person since our arrival on Neraka, and I realized it was largely because of him. He had a powerful effect on me, and I didn't like that, mainly because it felt like he was stealing away control of my otherwise cool temper. My friends called me the Cucumber back home for a reason, and I was slowly drifting away from that as the days went by and I remained on Neraka, remained so close to Caspian. I had a hard time recognizing myself, and I knew I had to get things under control.

I needed my head clear, my heart empty, and my stomach calm. But whenever my eyes met Caspian's, my insides were instantly ravaged by a category five storm. I missed the old me from a few days ago—calm and reserved, with scary-sharp reflexes, as opposed to the powder keg I'd become in just a few days of being on the same planet as Lord Kifo.

Thanks to the horses' speed, we reached the plain shortly after two in the morning. The field was pitch black around us, while the three moons lingered above, casting their warm light over us. The tracking spell glimmered and moved at a constant, slow speed.

Our search for Fiona had begun.

7

FIONA

(DAUGHTER OF BENEDICT & YELENA)

'd lost all notion of time passing since the moment the daemon had emerged from the pool and I had beheld him, in all his deadly glory, for the first time. Every one of my senses felt stunned. That red powder he'd blown in my face had relaxed my body a little too much, and the sight of him, so tall, dark, and dangerous, was permanently seared into my retinas. I took deep breaths, trying to get hold of myself. He walked over to the fire, settling on one of the stones and proceeding to sharpen his blades with a solid gray crystal.

I watched the sparks fly out as the crystal screeched down the sharp metal edge, while his red gaze occasionally darted my way. His long black hair was damp and pulled over one shoulder, getting wavy as it gradually dried.

"So you're a daemon," I managed finally, stating the obvious. "I'm guessing you're one of the many behind the abduction of Exiled Maras and Imen. You're a killer."

He didn't react, and kept his eyes fixed in front of him.

"What's your name? Where do you come from? Why did you start taking innocent people? What's your issue with Azure Heights?"

I didn't get any answers. Some minutes went by as I tried to figure out a better way to approach this, to get him to talk to me. I knew he understood me, and he was perfectly capable of coherent speech, as he'd so casually proven earlier.

I figured I'd try a less accusatory approach. "My name's Fiona. What's yours?"

It worked. He finally looked my way, his gaze finding mine. Then he stood and sauntered across the cave, closing the distance between us. He sheathed the dagger he'd been sharpening, letting it hang loosely on his belt. I froze, breathlessly waiting until he reached my cage.

He stopped in front of the iron bars, staring at me for a while. He said nothing, but I could see genuine curiosity in his red eyes, while his overall expression gave nothing else away. I dared to inch closer, my movement so slow and smooth, I hoped it would barely be noticeable. I didn't have any of my usual strength, my muscles and tendons weak thanks to his red powder trick. I realized I couldn't even extend my claws to use them as weapons against him. The only thing I could think to do was at least try to use my hands to grasp at the dagger.

I held his gaze while my right hand slowly reached for the blade on his belt, sneaking between the cage bars. I felt my temperature rise, then the rough fabric strip covering the dagger's handle as it brushed against my fingertips.

Another inch and it's mine.

He smirked, then gripped my left wrist and jerked me forward with a sudden pull. My face hit the iron bars, my cheek and temple pressed against the cold metal. His lips were just inches away from mine, stretched into a lazy grin that revealed his white teeth. My skin was broiling under his gaze, his fingers digging into my flesh as he held me in place. I didn't regret my attempt to grab that weapon off him, but I knew I'd gotten myself into serious trouble with that move.

I waited with bated breath, but he said nothing for about half a minute. He kept looking at me with a flicker of amusement in his eyes, while I pondered the many ways in which he could kill me in that moment. My stomach twisted into knots.

"I'm Zane," he announced, his voice once again making my nerves shudder.

Okay... so maybe he won't kill me just yet.

"I'd say it's nice to meet you, *Zane*, but we both know I'd be lying," I replied, unwilling to give him any kind of high ground—especially not moral. Sure, I'd just attempted to steal his knife after he'd fed me, but he was the one who put me in that cage in the first place. "Why am I here? Why did you take me? Why am I being kept in a cage like an animal?"

I overestimated his willingness to talk. His skin felt hot against mine, his breath tickling my nose. He didn't let go, but he didn't answer either. My only sliver of comfort was the cool iron pressing against my face.

"Why am I here? Why did you take me? Why am I being caged like this?" I asked again. I couldn't let him set *all* the rules. I had to get him to talk to me. I had to try to soften him up enough to convince him to let me go. Or at least keep him busy so I could find a way to escape.

Zane scoffed, then let me go, stalking back to the fire. I got a good view of his broad back, his muscles, sculpted to perfection, flexing with his movement. He sat down, resuming his blade-sharpening session.

"I haven't made up my mind as to what I'm going to do with you yet," he replied, his tone flat and somewhat bored. "But if you keep trying to escape, you'll make it easier for me to decide, and it won't help you, *Fiona*."

I pulled myself back, and noticed the tremor in my left hand. I glanced at Zane, who went on with his task, seemingly unimpressed by my demeanor. I had to get him to talk to me more. I had to get on his good side and in his head. I needed to find a way out of here, one way or another.

My team was surely out there, somewhere, searching for

me. I had to get to them before they ventured too deep into the gorge and got themselves hurt trying to find me. Besides, my own safety was hanging in the balance every minute I remained trapped in this cage. No matter how taken aback I'd been by Zane's appearance, and how calm his demeanor currently was, I couldn't trust a monster.

8

CAIA

(DAUGHTER OF GRACE & LAWRENCE)

We reached the Valley of Screams, the gorges rising before us like dark giants filled with deadly secrets. The wind rustled through the leaves of nearby trees, and a stream flowed on our left side, snaking its way through the tall glass. We followed it into the gorge, the tracking spell light hovering a couple of feet ahead of us.

Vincent and the Correction Officers were right behind us, their horses occasionally huffing and neighing. Ours did the same, most likely sensing the dangers hiding within the valley. The moons were bright and full, casting their diaphanous light in shades of yellow, orange, and white. It was enough for me to get a decent view of the narrow path ahead, through the gorge.

Sharp black walls rose on both sides, with shrubs and

dark green trees sprinkled along the way. The stream carved its way through, framed by rich, irregular patches of grass and wildflowers. Myriads of stars twinkled across the black sky, and I would have appreciated their beauty, and that of our general surroundings, much more were it not for the occasional distant scream echoing through the gorge.

My skin crawled whenever one pierced through the nocturnal silence. I was still recovering from our incursion into the Exiled Maras' prison, still shaken up by what had happened to Fiona. We'd seen what those daemons were capable of. We knew what could, and would, eventually happen to their victims. Captivity at the hands of those horned beasts yielded nothing but pain and death, and the idea of Fiona suffering the same fate as the others clawed at my heart.

"Caia, we'll get her back," Blaze said softly as he pulled his indigo horse closer to mine. My nerves were tight, my muscles stiff. All I could do was give him a weak half-smile, to acknowledge his attempt to reassure me.

"It was bad enough when I didn't know what the daemons looked like," I murmured. "Now that I've seen one, I can't help but quiver at the thought of Fiona captured by one of them. I know she's strong, and yes, she *is* a survivor, but I still dread her chances right now... I'll feel a lot better when we find her."

Harper, Jax, and Hansa were several feet ahead of us, followed closely by Patrik, Scarlett, Avril, and Heron, with

Blaze and me farther back. The presence of fifty Correction Officers behind us did make me feel a little bit better. At least our backs were covered, while we continuously scanned our sides and the path unraveling before us.

"I meant it, by the way... what I said earlier," Blaze said, a pained expression coming over his face. "I would have gone after her right then and there. It wasn't an easy choice to make."

"I know, Blaze," I replied gently. "In hindsight, it was better this way. We did the right thing by returning to the infirmary, because at least now we know what our enemy looks like. We know what we're going against, and, most importantly, we've learned how to bypass their invisibility. My only hope is that we're not too late..."

"I doubt it," Jax interjected, glancing over his shoulder at us. "Minah was kept in a cage before she escaped. I have a feeling these daemons don't feed on their victims in one go. It's only been a couple of hours, more or less. The trail is still hot. Don't let this eat away at your morale. We'll get her back, and we'll burn down this entire gorge if we have to."

Jax wasn't a Mara of many words, in general. He rarely spent time motivating us. He hated doing speeches and usually left Draven or Field to welcome new recruits into GASP. It meant something to hear him say those words to us, in that moment. It told me that he had hope, and that he didn't want us to abandon ours.

I felt a little more energized and straightened my back in

the saddle, my left hand holding the reins while the other played with one of my lighters, flicking it on and off. The tracking spell was slow and steady. We weren't close to Fiona yet, but I assured myself that it was only a matter of time.

There was suddenly movement ahead—a handful of shadows darting from left to right. We stilled, bringing our horses to a halt. My heart skipped a beat. Several wild animals resembling deer were scampering across the gorge. They stopped for a second to stare at us with their big, round brown eyes, before they disappeared into a nearby crevice. I breathed a sigh of relief, and we beckoned our horses to keep moving.

I heard Vincent's indigo horse trotting closer to us. I looked over my shoulder and noticed the wary look on his face, his eyes as big and round as those of the deer we'd just seen. Clearly, he wasn't cut out for this kind of expedition. He would've been better off selecting color palettes for some new wing in the mansion, but I did appreciate his eagerness to help. He had a soft spot for Fiona, and it was nice to see him act on it.

The Correction Officers behind him didn't look too comfortable either. Their heads kept turning, their eyes constantly scanning the gorge, one hand always clutching a sword handle. Cadmus was the most difficult to read—we'd been introduced to the leading lieutenant earlier, during our crossing of the plains. His expression was firm, a permanent frown pulling his dark brown eyebrows together over his pale blue eyes. It didn't look like anger, but it didn't exactly look like fear, either.

"Are you afraid?" I asked Cadmus, wondering if I'd get a reaction out of him.

"We have lost many people in these gorges," he replied stiffly. "Some were family; others were close friends. Of course we're scared. You must be either suicidal or stupid, or both, if you're not afraid right now."

Okay, not the friendly type. Got it.

"I didn't say I'm not scared," I said, staring ahead. "I can't speak for the rest of my team, but I've got chills running down my spine. That hasn't stopped me from coming down here to do the right thing, though."

"I agree," Cadmus replied. I didn't turn to look at him, but I heard his voice soften a little. "We have a mission; we have our orders and a duty toward our Lord Kifo, who commanded us to watch over you and your team."

"And it is much appreciated," Harper chimed in, pulling her horse's reins so she could move closer to the Mara lieutenant. My gaze followed her, watching her exchange with Cadmus. "Speaking of brooding marble statues, what's up with him? What's he like, as a commander?"

Cadmus let out a sigh, as if searching for the right words to describe Caspian—a struggle also indicated by the way in which he pursed his lips and averted his eyes.

"Lord Kifo is a mystery to most of us," he replied.

"Mostly because he lost his parents at a young age and was raised by Dillon, a family friend and trusted general of his House. Caspian was educated in a military environment and taught not to display his emotions. It became a part of his nature, I suppose. A lot of people in the city don't trust him, but that's purely because they don't know him. We tend to fear what we don't understand."

"Yeah, he doesn't exactly come across as... likeable," Harper muttered.

"Lord Kifo often disagrees with the other Lords, as well," Cadmus explained. "He's a dedicated servant of Azure Heights, and cares about our people, but his methods are usually questioned because of differences in ethics. Lord Kifo is not known for his mercy or compassion, and is very strict where our laws are concerned. That usually leaves room for disagreement and friction with the more progressive Houses ruling over the city."

"That's not true," Vincent intervened, slightly offended. "We like Lord Kifo, despite his abrasiveness. He's a valued member of our council and—"

"Why don't you stick to supervising your art department, milord?" Cadmus cut him off, visibly annoyed. He didn't seem to like Vincent much. Upon a second glance, none of the Correction Officers seemed pleased to be around him. "Clearly, you have very little understanding of the inner workings of the Lords. You know, since you're not a House ruler, nor were you ever educated to become one. Sienna was meant to take over House Roho, not you."

"Whoa, that's a bit harsh," Harper said, but Vincent didn't flinch.

"It's okay, Miss Hellswan," he said. "Cadmus is entitled to his opinion, just like everyone else. I don't have to like it, but I must respect it. It's part of our ethos as Exiled Maras. Brutal honesty is better than cheap acting, I always say."

"Glad you understand," Cadmus replied, undeterred. "I'm merely stating the obvious here. Vincent was never a part of any leadership decisions. If anything, Sienna was the one assisting Lady Roho during council meetings. It's just a fact. Now, however, unfortunately, the situation has changed, and Vincent is being groomed to take over House Roho one day, in the absence of his sister. But he still has a lot to learn about Azure Heights's leadership issues."

"Care to elaborate on these leadership issues, as you call them?" Harper asked, wearing a friendly smile. She wasn't one to show such warmth to strangers, leading me to believe that she was politely trying to drill the Mara lieutenant for information regarding the upper echelon.

Smart girl. Might as well, since we're here, and the Lords aren't.

"I'm not qualified to discuss it, really," Cadmus replied, but seemed to soften under Harper's gaze. "What I *can* tell you is that it has to do with the direction in which the city is going, more or less. Most of us want Azure Heights to stay here, while Caspian wants us to move, find a new, safer home. You could say he's a bit of a rebel, but he has valid reasons for his persistence. He feels that it would be easier if we start over elsewhere, rather than struggle with these... daemons here."

9

HARPER

(DAUGHTER OF HAZEL & TEJUS)

Cadmus wasn't exactly the most open of Maras, but he was certainly more useful and informative than Caspian, where Caspian was involved. The Mara lieutenant did help paint a better, clearer picture of Lord Kifo, but I still had a lot of unanswered questions.

Much to my dismay, most of these questions were of a personal nature, mainly because of the way I felt myself react whenever Caspian was around. I tried to convince myself that no question was too personal, given the mission at hand and the many unknowns surrounding it, but, still, I had to choose my words carefully so as not to draw any unnecessary attention.

"How well do you know Lord Kifo, on a personal level?" I asked in a low voice.

"I know him well enough," he replied with a shrug, looking ahead. I drew my horse a couple of feet closer to his, to encourage him deeper into the conversation.

"Okay, so I noticed he's very close to Amalia." I dropped my first non-question, wondering if he'd pick it up and help me figure out what was up with Caspian and Emilian's daughter. Sure, Rewa had told us about their betrothal and subsequent refusal to marry and unite Houses Kifo and Obara, but I knew I could get more information if I posed the right... non-question.

"Oh, those two have been friends since they were children," Cadmus said, smiling slightly. There was a twinkle in his eyes, and I wasn't exactly sure what it meant, other than familiarity. It made me think that Cadmus might have been around Amalia and Caspian as well, during their formative years, and that the twinkle was a sign of nostalgia for days gone by. "We grew up together, in fact. Dillon was my uncle, and he often invited my father and me to visit House Kifo. I spent many summers with Caspian and Amalia."

Nailed it!

"I can tell you one thing for sure," Cadmus continued, his head tilting as he listened to the near silence around us —the only noticeable sound was the water flowing on our left side. "Amalia is one of the few creatures in this city that Caspian has ever been affectionate toward. They were tapped for marriage, but said they would rather work to bring all Houses together and maintain their freedom, rather than unify two families and create some bourgeois monopoly over the Council. They're very good friends, though. Caspian would easily kill anyone who hurt Amalia in any way, but he's never shown any romantic interest in anyone. It was always platonic, downright brotherly with her. People often thought there was something between them but, *trust me*, there isn't."

The smirk he displayed at the end almost made me wonder if *he* had something going on with Amalia instead. I wasn't sure how relationships worked among the Lords and the "upper echelon". I didn't even know whether Amalia would be allowed to be with anyone she wanted, including a lieutenant of House Kifo, or whether her options would be limited to a handful of high-society Maras. Cadmus seemed like a solid guy; it would have been a shame not to let them be happy together.

"That being said," Cadmus added, giving me an intense stare—the kind that made my cheeks burn, as if I were the one student being singled out in class for a pop quiz, "it's been even more difficult to understand Caspian lately, particularly since GASP arrived here. His behavior has changed dramatically, and he's become very unpredictable."

For some reason, there was a pang of guilt digging its way through my stomach.

"What... Um, what do you mean?" I asked, my voice barely audible.

Do I have something to do with it? I mean, I do get a kick out of annoying him, but...

"He's undecided and foul tempered, mainly because of how you go against him, Miss Hellswan." He frowned. "I strongly advise that, going forward, you take his advice under consideration. He wishes GASP no harm whatsoever. On the contrary, he's looking out for your best interest."

"Right, by telling us to leave while your people are dying in these gorges?" I rolled my eyes, tired of hearing the same palaver regarding our capabilities as fighters and defenders of supernaturals.

"Is that what he told you?" Vincent asked, his eyebrows raised and his green eyes glimmering with curiosity.

"Oh, it's not important." I brushed him off lamely, feeling the conversation slowly drifting out of my control and into uncharted territory.

Vincent frowned, then shook his head slowly and looked away, as if mildly offended. There wasn't much I could do there, as I'd previously promised Caspian I'd keep the details of our conversations private, especially from the Exiled Maras.

I then noticed the glances from my team ahead, varying from inquisitive to confused. I exhaled sharply and gave them all a discreet shrug, knowing I'd have a lot of questions regarding Caspian to answer later. My explanatory note had barely done anything to explain his involvement in our mission or his knowledge regarding the daemons.

If anything, I now had more questions about him, and so did the others. And Caspian wasn't around to answer any of them. Not that he would've jumped to clarify anything, even if he were there. That guy required heavy-duty pliers when it came to getting him to divulge information... I seriously had to find a way soon, though.

Everything about this world was riddled with murky question marks, and I had a feeling that our survival and success in this mission, and my ability to anticipate what was coming next, depended on Caspian revealing whatever secrets he was guarding.

For now, however, I needed to focus on getting us out of this gorge alive.

10

AVRIL

(DAUGHTER OF LUCAS & MARION)

Our journey through the gorge was going suspiciously smoothly as we followed the small light orb that was Fiona's tracking spell. My stomach felt heavy as we advanced another mile, with just a few animal sightings here and there.

Harper was at the back, talking to Vincent and Cadmus, while Jax and Hansa led the way forward. I was right behind them, with Heron riding close to me. We'd barely spoken since we'd left the city—mostly because we were both strained, paying close attention to our surroundings, and anticipating a daemon attack.

"Knowing Fiona, she's probably kicking some daemon ass as we speak," Heron muttered, giving me a half-smile and a sideways glance meant to give me comfort. He'd seen me over the past couple hours; he'd sensed my anguish, and he was trying to make me feel better.

I couldn't stop myself from softening under his jade gaze. Our indigo horses trotted through the dark gorge, the three large moons glancing at us from the narrow strip of black sky above.

"Knowing Fiona, she's probably pulling daemons inside out like shirts hung out to dry," I replied with a smirk.

"Knowing Fiona, she's most likely having daemons for a very early breakfast." Heron kept going, pressing his lips together to stifle a grin.

"Knowing Fiona, I think we'll have to change the daemons' species name to 'rented mules'," I chuckled, feeling my spirits brighten. Jax had been right, earlier. We needed a soaring morale to get our uber-strong vampire girl out of this place, and Heron had the right formula.

"Knowing Fiona, she's probably doing a little bit of spring cleaning now, mopping the floor with those horned bastards," Heron continued.

"Knowing Fiona, and based on what I've seen on that dead daemon's head, I bet she's giving her captors some pretty nifty three-dollar haircuts." I giggled. His indigo horse huffed and moved closer, enough for Heron's knee to brush against mine.

"Knowing Fiona, she's probably smacking the taste of souls out of their mouths for good."

That last one made us both roar with laughter, but we

were immediately shushed by Hansa and Jax, while Scarlett, Patrik, Caia, Blaze, Harper, and even the Exiled Maras swallowed their chuckles.

"Keep it down! We're still in hostile territory," Hansa berated us with a hiss.

"Yeah, and so are the daemons around Fiona right now," Heron muttered, unable to help himself. I covered my mouth to stop myself from chortling, while Hansa gave him a reluctant grin and shifted her focus back to the road ahead. Even Jax noticed her expression, the corner of his mouth twitching in response.

We needed that laugh. It was a tiny slice of therapy in the middle of a madness that got more complicated and more dangerous with each hour that went by. Heron reached out, covering my hand with his. He gave me a gentle squeeze, his gaze softening as our eyes met. He energized me in ways I'd never thought possible, and that made everything about our friendship even more confusing, but in that specific moment, I welcomed it all. I needed it. I knew I'd worry about it later, since Heron hadn't changed. I'd still get my heart broken if I allowed myself to get too close.

"We're going to get her back, Avril," he said quietly, and I nodded. "And once this whole mess is over and we get back to Calliope, you and I are going to have a good, long talk."

His jade eyes took on a darker shade, his pupils dilating

as he noticed my lips slowly parting—something that happened instinctively whenever he came too close.

"A talk? About what?" I managed, following up with a dry swallow.

He blinked several times, then pulled himself back and frowned, as if he'd said too much.

"Um, stuff. Don't worry about it. It's... Let's just get out of here first." He gave me a nervous smile, before his head suddenly turned in the opposite direction. "Did you hear that?"

We all went silent and listened for a few seconds.

The water flowing by our side, murmuring over the rounded pebbles. The wind blowing through the trees, their leaves whispering throughout the gorge. A few small animals squeaking behind jagged slabs of limestone.

And a peculiar rumble that got louder and closer, expanding into a stomach-churning echo that prompted us to look up and witness the top sides of the gorge explode.

One loud bang was followed by three more, and the stone walls started collapsing. Massive rocks tumbled toward us.

Our horses jerked into action and darted forward. I heard shouting and muffled yelps behind us as the gorge broke down. Once the thunderous crashing noises stopped, we brought our horses to a halt and turned to look at what we'd escaped.

The way back was completely sealed. A thick, irregular

wall of broken chunks of limestone made it impossible for us to return that way.

Gray dust billowed out in heavy rolls, and the crash's echoes reverberated through nearby crevices. It quickly spread out above, obscuring the sky before it dissipated.

"What the hell was that?" I croaked, taking in a lungful of air. I'd been holding my breath from the moment the stones had hurtled down toward us.

"I don't know! The gorge simply... collapsed," Hansa gasped, nudging her horse with her heels. She got closer to the new wall, looking up and taking it all in, as Jax moved to her side.

It dawned on us then that our GASP team had been completely separated from Vincent and the Correction Officers.

"Crap. What about Vincent and the others?" I gasped.

"Vincent!" Hansa shouted. "Cadmus!"

A second passed before their voices, albeit low and muffled, could be heard from the other side. We all brought our horses next to Hansa and Jax, while Harper used her True Sight to look beyond the wall. The voices got clearer. I managed to identify Cadmus and Vincent—they were both alive.

"Vincent and Cadmus are okay," Harper said. "Some of the Correction Officers are wounded, but I think they'll recover."

"Vincent, Cadmus! Can you hear us?" Hansa called out.

"We can hear you," we heard Cadmus growl from the other side. "Keep moving forward—we'll go back and take one of the side paths into the next gorge, then find our way back to you farther ahead, okay?"

"Do you know where you're going?" Hansa replied.

"More or less, yes. We have a map, and we'll figure a way back to you. Keep moving, though! Don't be sitting targets for the daemons!"

"Did you see what happened up there?" Jax asked.

"No... No, we only heard the rumbling, then the whole thing came down!" Vincent answered.

"Yeah, they'll definitely be okay," Harper concluded as she continued looking through the wall. "They're getting back on their horses now."

"Don't fall back. Meet us farther up ahead!" Jax shouted.

"Relax, Dorchadas! We'll be right next door, so to speak!" Vincent shot back. Jax rose an eyebrow. He looked as though he were holding back a fine choice of curse words for the noble Mara.

"Look at him. Less than an hour out in the field and he's a freakin' warrior." Heron scoffed.

11

HARPER

(DAUGHTER OF HAZEL & TEJUS)

I watched as Vincent, Cadmus, and the Correction Officers turned back, their horses rushing and nervously neighing as the group looked for a path into the neighboring gorge. I couldn't neglect the knots in my stomach as I returned to my normal vision and gave Hansa a concerned look.

"I can't help but wonder if this was not accidental," I said.

She turned her indigo horse and proceeded to catch up with the tracking spell, now twenty yards away from us, and we followed.

"Have you seen anything in this world, so far, that went wrong and was just a coincidence?" Hansa replied, visibly annoyed by this unexpected turn of events. We were, after all, fifty-one men short.

"Nope, it's just one machination after another." I sighed, my instincts kicking in.

"We need to stay hyper-alert now," she said. "Whoever did this, they wanted us separated."

We were in enemy territory. We all knew what she meant by "whoever", and we were bound to see the air rippling around us soon enough. I couldn't see them, but my spine was tingling with anticipation. Daemons couldn't be far away.

"They blew up the gorge, though," Patrik said. "This means they're far better organized than we'd initially thought."

"Yes, and it also means they may be just as dangerous and skilled in battle without their invisibility gimmick as they are with it," Jax replied.

After following the tracking spell for another two hundred yards, my prediction came true.

The air rippled ominously before us as daemons emerged from nearby crevices. I heard their claws scratching against the stone, their feet shuffling around us.

"Get ready," Hansa growled, drawing her broadsword.

Our blades swished out of their scabbards, eager to take on the beasts closing in on us. Our horses stopped, shaking their heads and kicking their front hooves against the hard ground, as if warning the daemons to stay away. My mare in particular was a feisty one, her muscles jerking as I tightened my thighs against her ribs.

There were at least thirty of them, based on the flickers of red eyes that I could see, and they moved in a wide circle around us, looking for the perfect attack angle.

"Patrik, be a doll and do the honors, please," Hansa said, her glare fixed on a couple of fiends to her right.

The Druid nodded, then muttered a spell under his breath and put his left arm out, index and middle fingers pointing at the stream. The water burst upward, then spread out like rain, pouring all over us on a fifty-foot radius.

One by one, the daemons were revealed, shocked by this development. Their red eyes were wide, their mouths open —the only indicators of any emotion. Other than that, they were all designed to kill, just like the one back in the infirmary: they were extremely tall and robust, with razor-sharp claws and fangs, curved horns, and a plethora of tattoos covering various parts of their arms and chests.

They looked at one another for a moment, then scowled at us and began moving forward.

"Yeah, we broke their cover. They're not happy," I said, then patted my mare's neck. "Sorry, my friend, you need to step aside for this one. These guys are big and mean, and I don't want them to hurt you."

I got off and pointed to the side, where a dark and quiet corner could be used for cover. The rest of our team jumped off their horses as well. I used my mind control to push them aside.

"Go on, go wait for us there. We won't be long," I told my mare.

The creature neighed and trotted off to that corner, followed by the other horses. We then turned around and moved closer to the middle, gathering in a tight circle with our backs to each other. The daemons growled and prepared to pounce.

"These dudes are huge," Heron said, his sword out and thirsty for blood.

"It's a good thing we don't need any of them alive to lead us to Fiona." Scarlett glanced around, then shrugged. "I've been looking to intensify my practice, anyway."

"Let's just get this over with fast," Hansa replied, just as the first daemon smirked, then charged her. "The tracking spell keeps moving! Blaze, light 'em up!"

The rest of the fiends came at us at once.

But Blaze burst into full dragon form as soon as we made room for him, and the daemons were forced to scatter. The dragon was gorgeous, his black scales and dark orange underbelly rivaled only by his big, beautiful blue eyes, his clawed wings stretching out, and his spiked tail smashing left and right, into the fiends.

Some of the daemons evaded Blaze's claws and tail hits, but my twin swords didn't forgive. The horned creatures were ridiculously fast, though. Now that they were visible, they seemed even lighter on their feet, dodging my strikes left and right. I had two of my own to deal with, while Hansa, Jax, Scarlett, Avril, Heron, and Caia took on the others.

More daemons poured out of narrow slits in the stone walls, but Patrik's water shower kept coming down, and the Druid launched spheres of blue fire with his spare hand. They didn't kill the fiends, but they dazed them into standing still for long enough to get crushed between Blaze's jaws.

I avoided a direct hit from one of my two opponents, while Blaze turned and tried to get as many daemons as he could in one blow. We were too close and the gorge too narrow for him to use his fire, but he was big and angry enough to not give them a chance to bring any of us down.

A claw slashed my shoulder, and I hissed from the pain, then slid on my back with both swords up. I cut through a daemon's inner thighs, slipping between his strong, muscular legs. He roared from the pain, blood gushing on the ground in large crimson spurts, and I quickly jumped back to my feet and crossed my swords against the back of his neck. I cut his head off with one swift move, then took on another daemon.

I dodged its claws in a series of sidesteps, then brought my swords swishing through the air between us, the tips of my blades cutting deep into his forearms, then his chest and face. I kept hitting until the daemon was overwhelmed by the speed of my attacks. I caught a glimpse of our horses, and my blood froze, anger and bile rising into my stomach as I saw daemons tearing into them.

"No, no, no!" I growled, and drove my sword right through my opponent's throat.

He fell to his knees, and I kicked him back with my boot. I swerved through the clashes of swords and claws between Scarlett, Heron, and Avril, and ran toward the horses. Three were down, including my mare, blood pooling beneath them. My heart ached as I sidestepped one of the two daemons attacking the horses, and decapitated the one whose fangs had just pierced a fourth horse's throat.

The animal shuddered and managed to scamper off, while the other six moved farther back, unharmed and still under my control. I had a feeling the one that had just run off had snapped out after its injury.

I stumbled as a heavy kick landed in the small of my back. I managed to throw my arm back with one sword, but I missed the attacking monster by inches, and I left my side open for another attack. I saw his grin and his claws coming in for just that, when a wide blade pierced his neck from behind. He stilled, blood gurgling out of his open mouth, then fell flat on his face as the sword was withdrawn.

"What the—" I gasped, stunned to see Caspian standing before me, his mask and hood on, his jade eyes glimmering with fury, and his blade coated in daemon blood. I quickly glanced over his shoulder and saw a few more daemons coming, while the rest of my team killed their fair share, with Blaze still leading on the scoreboard.

"You'll get yourself killed. I told you!" Caspian spat, then turned around and took on a daemon.

A second fiend tried to get his side, while a third came at me. Even in such circumstances, Lord Kifo still found the time and energy to berate me.

The nerve of this guy!

My anger served me well, though, as I evaded a couple of attacks, then ran one daemon through with both my swords. I followed it up with a 360-degree turn to gather some speed and slashed the second daemon's side before it got a chance to hurt Caspian, who brought the other one down with a vertical gash, splitting his chest open.

"So, what, you've come along to die with us, Lord Kifo?" I said, gritting my teeth.

A couple more daemons scurried over their comrades' dead bodies to exact their revenge, but Caspian still found yet another second to further annoy me.

"No, I'm here to save you, because I've been raised to be merciful and helpful toward lesser creatures!" he shot back, then engaged the incoming daemons.

My blood boiled. But it was good fuel for what came next.

12

CAIA

(DAUGHTER OF GRACE & LAWRENCE)

My lighters were in full swing, setting incoming daemons on fire, enough to not only cause serious damage but also to give Scarlett, Heron, Avril, Hansa, and Jax the wiggle room they needed to cut them down.

Blaze was quite big for this part of the gorge, which didn't exactly work to our advantage, but he made the best of it, using the spike on his long tail and the sharp fangs in his strong jaws to wipe out daemons in clusters of two or three at a time. Yet more daemons were pouring through from the crevices, and it was beginning to feel like a never-ending stream of enemies by this point.

We stayed out of Blaze's way, while Harper and the newly arrived Caspian handled a string of daemons on their own.

It made me nervous whenever one got close to Blaze's head; they were offputtingly fast. Their clawed blows left large holes in the ground whenever I dodged them, and some threw knives at us between hits. It was slightly easier now that we could see them, but the daemons were twice as ferocious.

I put one lighter away and drew my sword, using one hand for a fire whip and the other to slash at the daemons trying to reach Blaze. I could see their red eyes fixed on his as they tried to move around and get better angles. Blaze's skin was tough, nearly impenetrable, but his eyes weren't. I lashed at the fiends while executing 360-degree turns to increase the speed of each hit, the incandescent tip of my fire whip taking hefty bites out of the daemons' flesh.

I blocked an attack with my sword, then slid down on one knee and directed a lash at a daemon dashing toward Blaze, who was busy stabbing several fiends before they reached one of the crevices. The fire whip burned through the daemon's thigh, enough to make him scream and for Blaze to turn his head to the right to see the beast, then impale him with his tail spike.

We didn't spot the other daemon, coming in hot from the left, until it was too late. He moved in a zigzag pattern, tapped his foot against a slab of limestone, and launched himself upward. He stabbed the corner of Blaze's left eye with his claw, and I screamed.

Blaze roared from the pain, making the entire gorge

shudder with echoes of his agony. He shook his massive head, enough to make the daemon fall to the ground with a thump. Jax rushed over and pierced the fiend's neck with both swords, cursing under his breath.

"Everybody back off!" I managed to shout. I saw Blaze's neck stiffen and swell as blood poured from his injured eye. It was about to get really hot for the twenty daemons left.

The team immediately reacted, dashing off to the sides. I pulled myself back several feet. Blaze growled and spat out a column of devastating fire over the remaining daemons. It happened fast. The creatures didn't stand a chance; Blaze's dragon flames rained down as liquid fire and obliterated every hostile in that part of the gorge.

Black smoke billowed from the daemons' charred remains as they disintegrated and scattered across the hard ground. Blaze then grumbled, his scales twitching as he shifted back to his normal form. He fell to his knees, one hand covering his left eye.

I ran to him, putting my sword and lighter away, while Harper and Caspian brought the remaining horses out. Jax, Hansa, Patrik, Heron, and Avril gathered around us, their swords out. They scanned the area for more hostiles, but it seemed as though we'd managed to survive our large-scale daemon attack.

My chest tightened as I lowered myself in front of Blaze. He was in pain, and had already broken out into a cold sweat, his face pale. Blood glazed his left cheek and trickled down. There was a puncture wound at the corner of his eye. Scarlett joined us, biting into her palm to open a gash for him to drink from.

"Hold on, Blaze," she said, then pushed her hand against his lips. "Drink."

Blaze drank some of her blood, while I rummaged through my backpack for bandages and Patrik gave him a healing pellet, along with a small, purple dried fruit.

"Eat this," the Druid said. "It'll help with the pain."

"Hold still," I said softly.

He obeyed, gritting his teeth, and put his hand down, revealing his injured eye. The eyeball had only been grazed, from what I could see, and it would heal faster with vampire blood and healing herbs from the Druid. It was red and a bit swollen, blood still trickling from the puncture wound. It hurt me on the inside to see him like this, but I took comfort in the fact that we'd been able to give him two effective treatments. Hopefully he'd be healed soon. I bandaged his eye, wrapping the thin fabric around his head, then wiped his cheek and neck.

He watched quietly as I cleaned the blood off his skin, then backed away. Heron handed him a pair of pants—we'd all packed spares in the satchels on our horse saddles, just in case. We knew there would be more than one instance in which Blaze would have to go full dragon in these gorges.

"Thank you." He gave me a weak smile, then nodded at Patrik and Scarlett.

"Thank *you*, Blaze." Hansa patted his shoulder. "You made our work much easier."

"Just take care of yourself," Jax added, gripping the reins of an indigo horse. "The daemons are twice as fast and vicious if they're visible, as we've all learned just now, and they will actively look for weaknesses. We need to be more careful, going forward. This won't be the last time they try to take a swipe at your eyes."

Blaze nodded, then stood up and slipped into his pants, while we all looked away. I couldn't stop my cheeks from flushing. Even in those circumstances, I seemed to be highly reactive to his presence and his body.

"At least we know we can beat them." Blaze shrugged, buttoning his pants.

"Now let's quickly address the elephant in the gorge." Harper raised an eyebrow, crossing her arms over her chest as she looked at Caspian, whose hood and mask were still on. "You can take those off, Lord Kifo. I already had to tell my team about you."

A few seconds passed as Caspian's jade eyes scanned us, followed by his head and shoulders dropping. He removed his mask and pulled the hood back, revealing himself with an irritated expression.

"Clearly, I cannot trust you to keep a secret," he muttered, resting one hand on the hilt of his sheathed sword.

"Not when you give me meranium pendants for the

whole team and expect me to figure out a good explanation," Harper replied.

"Harper hasn't told us much, other than the fact that you've helped us twice now, and also gave us the pendants to protect us against daemons trying to consume our souls." Jax frowned. "For that, we are obviously thankful. Rest assured that we won't tell anyone outside GASP about what you did for us."

"That being said," Hansa added, "we have a lot of questions for you. First off, what are you doing here?"

Caspian gave Harper a sideways glance, pursing his lips. He seemed genuinely cross with her.

"I figured you might need an extra pair of hands, and I was right. Had I not shown up, your sentry here would've been torn to shreds," he said.

"If I were you, I wouldn't jump to that conclusion, but thanks anyway," Harper retorted.

"Why are you helping us? What do you know about the daemons? What aren't you telling us about the Exiled Maras?" Hansa continued her drilling.

Caspian heaved a sigh, then looked around.

"I'm just going to tell you the same thing I told Miss Hellswan," he replied. "Get your vampire back, if you can. And then get out of Neraka. You are in over your heads, and there's nothing I could tell you to make it easier for you."

"And I'm just going to tell you what Harper has probably already told you," Hansa replied, her scowl highlighting the gold flakes in her emerald eyes. "GASP can help with what-ever is going on here, even on a large scale. Blaze is not the only dragon we have. You've seen us by now; you know we won't back off."

Caspian glanced briefly at Blaze, then gave Hansa a nod.

"Tell you what," he said, "if you make it out of this gorge alive, I'll reconsider your offer to help. Until then, however, your focus should be on your survival and on getting Miss Achilles back, not on my knowledge or motives regarding all this. I imagine Miss Harper has already explained that I do not seek to obstruct your investigation, nor do I wish to harm you. We seem to be, more or less, headed toward the same objective, which is the salvation of my people. But I cannot trust you. Not right now. Not until I see what you're really capable of. This daemon scuffle was light. You've seen them, now. You know what they're capable of. There is worse to come. Prove yourselves. Survive this mission and we'll talk. In the meantime, however, I must stress the importance of withholding my involvement from anyone outside this group. Innocent lives depend on it."

"Fair enough," Jax replied, then patted his horse's neck. "We need to go now. The tracking spell is still moving."

We all looked ahead, and saw the light orb hovering a third of a mile away.

"We're short on horses, though," Patrik muttered, grip-ping the reins of another indigo mare. There were six left, and more of us.

"I'll take one," I said, then looked at Blaze. "You can ride with me. This way, you'll have some time to heal."

I got on one of the horses, and Blaze swiftly joined me, climbing behind me. I pulled on the reins and directed the creature toward the tracking spell. Patrik took Scarlett on his horse, while Jax and Hansa reluctantly shared her mare. Avril and Heron each had their own, with one stallion left for Harper and Caspian.

Blaze's warmth simmered through me as he wrapped one arm around my waist for support. My breath hitched when he tightened his hold on me, his lips by my ear.

"Thank you, Caia," he whispered.

I blushed and thought about a response, but the only thing I could come up with was a faint nod. He slowly leaned against my back, gradually relaxing in the saddle. Our horse trotted forward, the motion seriously not helping, as each movement somehow made Blaze slip even closer, his thighs rubbing against mine in the process.

Well... This is going to be an interesting ride.

13

HARPER

(DAUGHTER OF HAZEL & TEJUS)

While the rest of my team split between horses, I found myself awkwardly standing on my own. Caspian pulled the last horse around and motioned for me to get on it. I was equal parts annoyed and relieved to see him, and that didn't sit well with me. My heart felt tight against my ribs whenever our eyes met, and my pulse kept jumping at the sound of his voice. Then my blood boiled as soon as he opened his mouth to talk down to me. Rinse and repeat.

"Get on," he said impatiently.

"Nah, I'm good." I shook my head and turned to join the rest of my team. "I can walk, or get on Avril or Heron's horse."

"Don't be foolish." Caspian rolled his eyes and let out an exasperated sigh. "I won't bite. Now get on."

I wasn't thrilled with being so close to him, but it was too late to object, as the team was already advancing through the gorge at a higher speed to catch up with the glowing tracking spell.

"Fine, but I'm leading," I muttered, and got on the horse, tying my backpack to the saddle's side.

Caspian climbed behind me and snatched the reins from my hand. "No, you're sitting in the front because I'm much bigger than you. *I'm* leading."

He didn't give me a chance to reply to his dominant assertion. His arm tightened around my waist and pulled me closer into him, while his spare hand guided the horse. He clicked his teeth and nudged the animal's ribs, prompting it to rush after the rest of my team.

I tried to breathe in a normal fashion, but his grip on me was firm, and his head slowly inched forward over my right shoulder. His chin brushed against my temple. I realized exactly how tall and well-built he was, with nothing but hot muscles covering my back, beneath layers of fabric. His scent tickled my senses, an intense mixture of musk and wild roses, reminding me of midsummer nights in The Shade, somehow, and the simple pleasure of basking in the moonlight.

Several minutes went by—minutes I spent trying to form eloquent or at least coherent thoughts, while his heartbeat echoed against my shoulder blades, his hot breath tickled my skin, and his thighs brushed against mine.

"I must admit, I'm equal parts dismayed and impressed by your stubbornness and persistence in staying here, on Neraka, while everything in this gorge is eager to kill you," Caspian said, his husky voice trickling into my ear and rumbling through my chest.

"At least you're entertained," I muttered. "Looking on the bright side, here."

"I am, yes. I'm also curious to see whether you all make it out of here alive or not," he replied, and I gave him a sideways glance. His jade eyes were burning holes through me. I shifted my focus back to my team and the path ahead. The stream gently rolled toward the eastern plain, several miles behind us.

"Glad to hear you're having fun."

"If you succeed tonight, you might actually be able to help," he whispered, his cheek brushing against mine as he lowered his head, and the horse briefly jerked to the side. I felt Caspian's body stir and tighten with the movement, his arm pressing into my stomach. I exhaled sharply, and he brought his head even lower, to the point where his eyes were on the same level as mine and my skin simmered all over. "Neraka doesn't want you to survive, and it will do everything in its power to stop you."

"You talk about the planet like it's a single entity," I

managed, trying to keep my breathing under control and not let Caspian know how much he affected me.

"In many ways, it is," he replied, then straightened his back.

I looked around, seeing the gorge with new eyes. Instead of taking its various elements separately, as pieces of natural architecture—the limestone walls, the dark crevices, the stream, the wild animals, and the daemons—I took them as parts of a whole. A single, unified organism with an objective.

And it gave me the chills, as I sensed the natural hostility. I didn't belong here, and Neraka seemed to know it.

Every inch of this place probably wanted to kill me. Or worse, feed on my soul.

14

HARPER

(DAUGHTER OF HAZEL & TEJUS)

We caught up with the tracking spell and continued to follow it, quietly and cautiously, through the gorge. Its speed was still quite slow, but I hoped it was only a matter of time before we'd see it dart toward wherever Fiona was being held captive.

I grew mildly accustomed to Caspian's body, in the sense that his strong torso provided me with comfortable back support—I'd leaned into him, gradually relaxing and hoping he wouldn't notice. He didn't seem to mind, and, since he was the one with the reins, I took the time to analyze our surroundings and use my True Sight to look through the walls.

There were only animals scurrying through neighboring gorges and no sign of Vincent or the Correction Officers. The strip of sky visible above was an intense black sprinkled with stars, and one of the moons looked down on us, the other two hidden beyond the gorge's walls.

I was feeling a little drained, and it dawned on me then that the last time I'd fed it had been off Blaze, on our first day here. It usually took more than two days for me to tap out, and I could tell, from my True Sight range at that point, that the daemon fight had left its mark on my energy levels.

As much as I'd disliked the idea of being so close to Caspian prior to riding the horse together, I was relieved that he was there. I could actually relax for a handful of minutes, before checking to see if any of my teammates would spare some energy for me. My worst-case scenario involved syphoning off the next hostile headed my way, but that sounded like quite the mission. Daemons were far more interested in killing me than standing by for my sentry nourishment.

"What's wrong with you?" Caspian asked me.

"Huh? What do you mean?" I mumbled, my gaze fixed on the tracking spell hovering ahead.

"You're getting soft," he replied. He then lowered his head, his lips tickling my earlobe and sending electric impulses down my spine. "If I didn't know any better, I'd think you were trying to flirt with me, with the way you're melting in my arms."

"Wait, what? No!" I blurted, and immediately sat up

straight, startling our horse. The creature shuddered, and I wound up being tilted back into Caspian.

I tried to move again, but his hold on my waist tightened, keeping me firmly gripped against his torso.

"I didn't say I disliked it," he murmured, further lighting my senses on fire.

Was he toying with me? Was he being sarcastic? Was there an endgame here?

"Nothing like that, Lord Kifo," I replied through gritted teeth. "I'm just a little weak, that's all. Trying to save my energy. I'm a double-trouble when it comes to feeding. I need blood for sustenance, and I need mental energy from creatures around me to keep my sentry side sated and capable of creating strong barriers and accurate True Sight."

"Barriers... You mean the pulses you were pushing out earlier?"

"Yes. They're concentrated energy waves." I sighed, once more softening against him and secretly hating myself for it.

"Tell me more about your sentry abilities," he said.

With nothing better to do, I obliged. I figured he'd be more open with me if I told him more about myself, hopefully establishing a two-way trust channel with the Mara who knew most about this place.

"Sentries are creatures that developed from humans after spending too much time around ghouls," I explained briefly. "Humans are a lot like your Imen, if that makes sense. Sentry abilities are mostly mental. We can syphon

energy off other creatures, which is how we sharpen our
sentry senses. We can read emotions. That's kind of like
reading minds, to an extent. Some of us can see through
pretty much any surface with True Sight. We can even
mind-meld, which can be best described as two souls merg-
ing, feeling and sensing each other at all times. It's very intimate, usually done by couples. And we have some mind-
control abilities as well, though not as strong as the Maras',
from what I've seen so far."

Several moments passed as Caspian seemed to process
my brief description of sentry abilities. He cocked his head
to one side, turning it slowly to better look at me, curiosity
glimmering in his jade eyes.

"Can you read my emotions?" he asked, his voice low.

I shook my head in response, trying to hide my disappointment. My life on Neraka would've been much simpler,
had I been able to read a Mara's emotions. We might have
even solved this mystery by now.

"That's a shame," he muttered. "And you need energy
from living creatures to strengthen your barriers and hone
your meddlesome vision..."

"Yeah," I replied, ignoring his jab regarding my True
Sight. He was still holding a minor grudge for the way I'd
seen through his mask, earlier in the night. "Normally I'd
ask Caia or Blaze, since he's a dragon and has tons to spare,
but Caia's in the middle of this with us, and Blaze is recovering from his injury, so I'll have to tough it out till later. I'm

still perfectly functional, but I'll perform much better once I syphon some energy. My bet's on the next daemon I cross paths with, assuming I'll manage to hold him down for long enough to feed off him, then kill him."

Another minute went by in silence before Caspian spoke again.

"Would you like to syphon some energy from me?" he asked, making my stomach drop.

My head whipped around so I could look at him, and I instantly found myself locked in the pale green pools of his eyes. Judging by his expression, he was serious. My heart skipped a beat as my sentry hunger kicked in hard, and I started wondering what it would be like to let his energy flow through me. My lips parted slowly, and his gaze dropped to them. I tried to get my brain to catch up with my mouth.

"I-I'm not sure that's necessary, Lord Kifo," I croaked. "Surely, you need your energy, too, given where we are right now. I'll manage till later."

"Don't underestimate me, Miss Hellswan," he replied, still staring at my lips. It was odd and confusing, much like everything else about him. It was like he was showing me a different side of him, one I didn't know how to approach just yet. "You must feed now. Your sentry abilities are clearly an advantage against the daemons and against this entire damn gorge. Your team needs you at full strength. Syphon whatever you need off me. I'll be fine."

I mulled it over for a couple of seconds. Could I even feed off a Mara? I'd never tried it before. I didn't even think it would be possible, given how mentally cut off their species was from me. I couldn't read their emotions, nor could I influence their minds. However, I was curious, and figured it was a good time to answer that question. Besides, he was right. I needed my sentry game back on.

I nodded and allowed myself to relax. His arm still rested around my waist, and I tilted my head back, leaning it against his shoulder. I brought my hand up and placed it over his, intrigued by the electrifying sensations buzzing through my fingertips as soon as our skin touched.

I felt his entire being open before me, and my body instantly reacted to his energy pouring into me, to the waves of cool green that matched his eyes and filled me up like fresh mountain air. A muscle twitched in his jaw as he carefully examined my face, while I syphoned off him and felt the blood rush through me with the strength of a waterfall.

Caspian was an interesting specimen, to say the least, brimming with energy and strength I'd rarely seen. My entire being hummed, my hand gently clutching his before I realized that I was losing myself in him. I moved to sit back up, but he swiftly tightened his hold and beckoned me to stay exactly there, my back against his chest and my head on his shoulder.

"Feeling better?" he asked.

I nodded, not sure whether I should look away or keep

gazing at him. He was beautiful, the blade of his nose casting a shadow over his left cheek, his soft lips dangerously close to my face. His energy was not to be underestimated, either. It fueled me in more ways than one—both physically and mentally, strengthening my resolve. At the same time, it rattled me to think that there was a little bit of Caspian flowing through me.

He pulled me even closer, then focused on the road ahead. I could hear his heart thudding in his chest. There was more darkness and danger waiting for us in that gorge. Fiona was in there, somewhere. But for that brief moment in time, I was fine with just being there, on that horse, in Caspian's arms, sated with his energy.

I'd worry about his rattling effect on me later.

15

FIONA

(DAUGHTER OF BENEDICT & YELENA)

I had no way of knowing for sure, but I estimated at least an hour had passed since I'd first heard Zane speak. He was lounging by the steaming pool, relaxing against the pile of animal furs. He threw me occasional glances but ignored my every question.

In the meantime, I'd analyzed my cage, every hinge and iron bar, the lock and the distance to my weapons, which were discarded on the floor several feet away. I'd caught glimpses of moonlight hitting a cave wall on the left, closer to the exit. I'd formulated a pretty good idea as to what I could do to get myself out of there. That red powder's effects wouldn't last forever, and I sure wasn't going to let the daemon know when I was feeling sturdy again.

But my inability to fight back or even escape at this point didn't sit well with me. It frustrated me, and, as a result, I kept tossing and turning in my cage, letting out the occasional huff. Zane wasn't fazed by my increasing anxiety. If anything, I had a feeling he was getting a kick out of it. Leave it to Fiona to get herself abducted by a sociopath with a hot body, legs for days, and horns that could tear her apart in an instant. My current situation was mind-boggling.

"Seriously, though," I said, breaking the silence, "my team will come looking for me, and you *will* be better off if you let me go now, and just stay back."

He chuckled, his foot sinking slowly into the hot water. It was better to see him react like that than ignore me.

"Rest assured, Fiona, I am not impressed," he replied, his red gaze lingering on the turquoise pond as he moved his leg through it, "given how easy it was for me to take you in the first place. Though I'll admit, I did not see the dragon coming. I've never seen dragons before; I've only heard about them in old folk tales, but that doesn't change anything. It can still be killed. *Everything* can die. Even a dragon."

He looked at me intently as he said that. I sat up, leaning against the iron bars on my right, as my arms were still weak and not able to fully support the weight of my upper body.

"You got lucky because of your stupid invisibility trick!" I shot back. "How do you do that, by the way? Is it natural? Is it magic of some kind?"

"You're in over your head, Fiona." He smirked, stretching his arms out like a lazy cat. "I can tell from the questions you ask that you have absolutely no idea what you've gotten yourself into. I don't even know whether I should bother to tell you anything or not, considering how fast you'll all die here. Damn, I'm still trying to figure out whether I should laugh or feel sorry for you."

"Go on, try me," I hissed, failing to keep myself composed before his blatant arrogance. "At least I won't die stupid."

"Trust me, beautiful," Zane threw me a playful wink, further confusing me, "if I tell you what's going on here, then I'll definitely have to kill you."

Despite the chill running down my spine, I found a splinter of hope in his statement. It left me under the impression that he had yet to decide whether he'd spare or end me.

"Therefore, you're not at all inclined to kill me, am I right?" I decided to test that theory.

Within a split second, Zane stood in front of my cage. He'd moved so fast, I barely saw him until his face was once again inches from mine, startling me. I yelped and fell backward against the iron bars. The corner of his mouth twitched. His eyes glimmered bright red as he measured me from head to toe.

"I haven't decided yet," he replied with an underlying

growl. "For now, I'm very curious as to what your soul might taste like, because you are quite the firecracker!"

He inched even closer, his hand slipping between the bars. His arm was long enough for his fingers to reach me and brush a solitary lock of hair from my face. My skin felt tingly all over. I held my breath as he cocked his head to one side.

"I have never met anyone almost as strong as I am," he muttered. "Not even among my kind. I'm a bit of an anomaly. I didn't even know your strength until I grabbed you and you held your own to the point where I nearly lost you on my way out. You could easily defend yourself against most daemons, and that, beautiful, gives me all kinds of feelings."

His grin had a peculiar effect on my stomach. It felt as though rocks were tumbling inside me. I tried to keep my chin up and stay prepared to fight off any attempt he might make at consuming my soul. But I was stuck in this small cage, at his mercy.

"That's just so... creepy," I replied, raising an eyebrow. I couldn't let him smell my fear.

He chuckled, then moved away from the cage, resuming his lounging position by the pond, his hands under his head.

Some time passed before mellow heatwaves proceeded to wash over my muscles. With each minute that went by, I felt my body slowly regain its strength.

Hope blossomed in my chest. All I had to do was hold

on in here, and wait for Zane to go out so I could pull the cage bars apart and sneak out. The red powder's effect was finally wearing off.

16

AVRIL

(DAUGHTER OF LUCAS & MARION)

The gorge widened ahead into a large, circular space, before tightening its limestone walls again. It was an eerie place, completely different from what we'd seen so far. It looked like a hidden slice of paradise, with a deep pond of turquoise water carved in the middle. The stream passed through it, making the surface constantly ripple.

The pond alone was downright breathtaking. A plethora of luminescent underwater plants grew at the bottom, glowing white and casting their pale light against the smooth walls of the pond. Its edges were dressed in bright pink-and-yellow orchids, in a beautiful contrast with the pale blue ferns and fuchsia wildflowers scattered around the gorge. I craned my neck to take it all in, from the patches of crude green grass to the tops of the tall palm trees with large, waxy leaves that obscured the purplish dawn sky. It brought a smile to my face—it was so different from the stark wilderness of the Valley of Screams.

"This is beautiful," I mumbled, gazing around as we moved forward.

"If it weren't for the bloodthirsty daemons lurking around, I would totally recommend this as a picnic spot," Scarlett quipped from behind, making me chuckle—until I caught sight of the air rippling to my right.

"Guys, daemon—" A heavy blow cut me off as an invisible daemon knocked me off my horse. I fell on one side, the air pushed out of my lungs. Everything grew fuzzy. I heard neighing, Patrik's shout, then the sounds of water splashing and swords being drawn from their sheaths, before my vision cleared.

I jumped to my feet and saw the daemon, his claws and fangs extended as he fought Heron, who'd already jumped off his horse with his blade out. Harper pushed out a barrier, and the daemon wobbled on his feet.

I drew my sword and supported my weight on my left foot, getting ready to jump and run my blade through him. The daemon was fast, blocking Heron's hits, but he was no match for Harper, who came from behind and slammed another barrier right into the back of his head.

"No!" A woman's scream suddenly pierced the night, and the daemon fell forward, landing on his forearms with a grunt. "Don't kill him!"

We all stilled, our blades pointed at the beast.

A young female Mara came out from behind a colorful bush, wearing a long, delicate white cotton dress.

"What the hell?" Hansa gasped as the Mara scurried toward us and fell to her knees, shielding the daemon with her arms and upper body.

"Holy crap," I croaked, recognizing her long ginger hair and pale green eyes, her cupid's bow lips and full cheeks from the painting in the Roho mansion. "Sienna..."

"Wait, what?" Harper panted, her twin swords now aimed at both the daemon and Sienna. Her expression echoed our collective astonishment, as we all gaped at the odd couple before us.

"Sienna, of House Roho," I managed.

"Vincent's sister," Heron confirmed, nodding slowly. His gaze darted between her and the daemon.

"Please don't hurt Tobiah," Sienna cried out, tears streaming down her face. The daemon straightened his back and wrapped his arms around her in a protective gesture. He gave us a wary frown, flinching from the pain caused by Harper's last barrier. "He was just trying to protect me!"

We ran out of words at the sight of Sienna so close to a daemon.

She'd been reported missing by her mother and brother. We'd thought she was a victim, abducted by the same daemons that had taken the others. We'd also suspected she might have been kidnapped by someone inside Azure Heights, given that her disappearance didn't match the daemons' original pattern. We'd floated several theories regarding her whereabouts, and yet... here she was, hidden inside the gorge and showing affection toward one of the very fiends we were hunting.

What is going on?

17

HARPER

(DAUGHTER OF HAZEL & TEJUS)

"Explain yourself, Sienna," Hansa barked, "before I run my sword through both of you!"

Sienna's green eyes grew wide with horror. Jax groaned, then placed his hand on Hansa's blade, lowering it.

"She's not going to do that, Sienna, don't worry," he said calmly, then gave the succubus a stern look. Hansa wasn't having it, though.

"Are you kidding? After what she put us and her family through?" Hansa retorted, then gave Sienna a cold glare. "Explain yourself, Sienna. Your family thinks you're dead. You're part of the reason we got dragged into this daemon mess. And you're here, living it up with one!"

"I'm sorry!" Sienna cried out. "I truly am! But... But Tobiah won't hurt you, I promise! Please, spare him!"

"Okay, okay, let's do this the right way," Jax replied, putting his sword away. "The daemon stays down while we have a quick conversation, and you take a few steps back. We don't know anything about you and the creature at this point, and we want to make sure you're safe."

"I *am* safe! Tobiah would never hurt me," Sienna sobbed.

Jax motioned to Hansa, prompting her to put her sword away, as well. She didn't seem happy to do it, but I figured they wanted Sienna calm and separated from the daemon, in case things went south fast. The young Mara may have claimed that Tobiah wouldn't hurt her, but Jax didn't want to risk giving him such an opportunity. We didn't know enough about the daemon to stop considering him an enemy. I'd been around Jax for long enough to understand how his judgment worked.

I looked toward the tracking spell. It was still moving slowly. We could spare a few minutes here, and we clearly needed to make some sense out of what we were seeing with Sienna and her daemon.

"Sienna, move away from Tobiah," Hansa instructed. "We won't hurt him if we don't have to, I promise. Just do this for now, for our peace of mind."

Sienna wiped her tears with the sleeve of her dress, then pushed herself up and took a couple of steps back, her gaze fixed on the daemon, who stayed down on his knees. He looked around at us, his red eyes glimmering slightly, as if carefully analyzing us. He was handsome, by all possible standards, his horns, a dark shade of gray, creating an interesting contrast with his long, ash-blond hair.

He retracted his claws and fangs, his shoulder dropping slowly as he seemed to accept the fact that he was outnumbered.

The moons had set by now—shortly after our latest daemon scuffle—and the sun was preparing to rise, somewhere east of the gorge. We pulled our hoods over our heads, preparing to shield ourselves from the first rays. Patrik, Caia, and Blaze were spared this daily ritual—not that it bothered me much, as vampirism came with some exquisite perks. Sienna noticed, as she pulled her own hood and frowned at the three.

"What are you?" she asked.

"Druid, fire fae, dragon," Hansa replied, pointing at each of them. "Now, talk to us, Sienna. What's going on here?"

"Dragon... I've only heard of dragons in old tales... Who are you people?" the Exiled Mara replied, biting her lower lip. Her jaw dropped when Caspian approached, his expression darkened slightly by the hood pulled over his head. "Caspian..."

"These are people from Eritopia. They were brought here to help find our missing people. Including you," Caspian said. "It would be wise of you to tell them what you're doing here with a daemon, while your mother and brother are losing their minds, believing you are dead."

"From Eritopia?" Sienna's eyes widened with surprise as she looked at us. She gave Tobiah a warm glance and a reassuring nod. "I'm sorry, I'm just shocked that you all made it this far into the gorges. This is a very dangerous place."

"No kidding," I shot back, sarcasm dripping from my tone. I put my swords away and crossed my arms over my chest. Heron and Avril kept their blades out and aimed at Tobiah, while Scarlett, Patrik, Caia, and Blaze sheathed theirs.

"Sienna, it really doesn't matter that we made it all the way here. We're professionals, and we're trained for this." Jax scoffed. "What really matters is why *you're* here, and not at home with your family and friends."

Sienna let out a long, tortured sigh, one hand playing with a lock of her hair, nervously twisting it around her fingers.

"I'm not going back home," she stated, then gazed around the gorge with a dreamy look in her eyes. "This is my home, now."

"The gorge. The Valley of Screams. The place where hundreds of your people have gone missing and were most likely killed." Hansa gave her a disparaging smile.

"It's where Tobiah lives. And I'm in love with him," Sienna retorted, unfazed. "I'm here for him. Because I want to be here with him."

Several moments passed as we glanced at each other, then stared at the daemon kneeling in front of us. To say that this was unexpected would have been an extreme understatement.

"You've been gone for over a week, and you're in love with a daemon?" I asked, recalling the timeline of Sienna's disappearance. "How do you even know about the daemons when the whole city, more or less, has no idea what they are?"

Sienna wore a sheepish smile and gave Caspian a brief glance before looking at me.

"I didn't know who or what they were either, until I met Tobiah," she mumbled. "Our people have been vanishing for two years now. My family was already a pain to deal with, so strict and stupidly superficial... With all the disappearances, it just made life even harder for me. I felt like I was living in a cage. I wasn't allowed to go out after sundown, which was ridiculous because I'm a Mara. Of course I need to be out after sundown! But I never planned for any of this to happen, I swear. It just happened! A few months ago, Tobiah showed his face to me while I was in my gazebo..."

I blinked several times, trying to picture that scene— Sienna lounging in her gazebo behind the Roho mansion, and an invisible daemon simply coming up to her. I couldn't help but imagine an eagle swooping down and grabbing an unsuspecting rabbit. Except, in this case, the rabbit seemed to have the hots for the eagle.

This is a whole new level of weird...

"I don't... I can't quite wrap my head around this," Hansa replied, scowling at the daemon.

"If... If I may?" Tobiah slowly lifted a hand, politely requesting permission to speak.

Jax raised an eyebrow, then gave him a brief nod.

"It's all my fault," Tobiah said.

"Understatement of the day." I snorted. Caspian shifted closer to me, his arm gently brushing against mine.

"I first noticed Sienna on the first level of the city," Tobiah continued. "I'd been prowling all night, looking to feed—"

"Eat a soul, you mean," Hansa interrupted him.

A muscled twitched in the daemon's jaw, but he kept a straight face as he went on.

"Yes, I was looking for a soul to eat," Tobiah replied. "Sienna was there, laughing with some Imen girls. I... I couldn't stop watching her. At first, I wanted to feed on her. She looked so beautiful under the moonlight, I kept wondering what her soul would taste like—"

"What *does* a soul taste like?" I asked.

Tobiah looked at me, a half-smile stretching his lips.

"It's like drinking liquid sunshine," he replied. "Happiness filling your mouth and lighting up your soul. It's incredibly addictive, and it does things to your body. You get stronger. Faster. Smarter."

"Like a nuclear battery," Avril muttered from the side.

"So you took Sienna." Hansa brought the conversation

back on track, while Jax motioned to Heron and Avril to put their swords away. There were too many of us against Tobiah. He wouldn't stand a chance in these circumstances if he did try anything.

"I did, but only because she wanted to come with me," Tobiah said, giving Sienna a look filled with longing and affection. "The night I first saw her, I followed her up to the mansion. I watched her for a while, and... Well, I couldn't take it anymore. There was a small spring gushing down the mountain, so I washed up and revealed myself to her."

I gave Caspian a sideways glance and noticed how calm and unfazed he appeared, while the rest of us were struggling to keep our eyes from popping out of our heads as Tobiah-the-freaking-daemon and Sienna told us their love story.

"You don't look surprised at all, Lord Kifo," I murmured. "Did you know all this?"

He gave me a bored look, slowly shaking his head.

"You really shouldn't rely on my facial expressions as indicators of any emotions or knowledge that I might possess, Miss Hellswan. I was trained in a military fashion. You can't read me like you do others. And to answer your question, no. I had no idea." He scoffed.

"I'll figure you out eventually," I muttered, narrowing my eyes at him before refocusing on Sienna and Tobiah. "So, what, you swooned and negotiated a happily ever after?"

"No! Not at all!" Sienna giggled. "I was terrified of him at first. At least, for the first few days. He kept coming around afterward, every night, without exception. He brought me blood to drink. He kept me warm. We got to know each other better, and... I fell in love."

"So you ran away with him, I presume," I interrupted.

"Well, yes." Tobiah shrugged. "I couldn't be with her in Azure Heights, and she couldn't exactly pack her bags and leave her family behind. They would've used her as bait to draw me out, then kill me. She's everything to me. She's the only creature in this world whose soul I don't want to consume. I want to cherish it because it's beautiful, and her family, her city... They're not worthy of it. I feel it in her smile, in the way she looks at me. It's precious..."

"I let Tobiah snatch me from the gazebo a week ago," Sienna added, smiling at the daemon. "And he gave me freedom."

"Then why didn't you send word to Azure Heights to at least tell your family that you're still alive?" Hansa asked.

"You don't *know* my family the way I do," Sienna replied. "They would've found a way to keep me away from Tobiah. Even worse, they would've tried to hurt him or kill him. I was tired of all the rules and etiquette, anyway. I like it here. It's simple, and wild, and it's our home. We're away from everything and everyone, and we only have each other... I wouldn't have it any other way."

"The other daemons think she's my prey, and they keep

their distance," Tobiah explained. "I've fought plenty of them off to keep this part of the gorge safe."

"And yes, my family thinks I'm missing," Sienna added. "I'd be more comfortable if they thought I was dead. It's better for everyone, because I could never go back to Azure Heights. Not now, after I've experienced bliss in Tobiah's arms..."

"This is getting a little too sweet for my taste," Heron muttered, awkwardly scratching the back of his head.

"Sweet? How about crazy? Unfathomable? Weird?" Avril chimed in, still having difficulties with this unconventional couple.

"Well, we are happy here." Sienna held her chin up. "Sure, it gets dangerous, and Tobiah has to fight some of his own people to keep me safe, but we're together. And no one in Azure Heights will ever understand."

"Okay, so, I got the lovey-dovey part down," Hansa replied bluntly, then moved closer to Tobiah. "Get up."

Tobiah obeyed and stood, and suddenly we were all quite short by comparison. He'd been on his knees for long enough to make us forget exactly how big he really was. He made Sienna look like a fragile little creature, the top of her head barely reaching his chest.

"Tell us about your daemons," Hansa continued. "What do they want? What are they doing here? Why are they taking people? What's their play?"

"The gorges are part of our hunting grounds," Tobiah

explained. "We have caves, where we feed and store our bigger game, all over the Valley of Screams. Daemons don't actually live here. Our world is deep underground... We like it hot, you could say, in the dark corners and volcanic flames beneath the surface of Neraka. This is just one of our favorite hunting areas. Daemons don't want anything in particular, other than to live our lives and hunt at leisure. We feed on souls, but, if we can't get any, raw meat will do, although we need to eat more often if we don't consume souls."

"Is that why you're taking people? Exiled Maras and Imen alike?" Jax asked.

"Yes." Tobiah nodded slowly. "A single soul can keep us sated for days. We don't like coming to the surface too often. I'm one of the few exceptions who like it here. Anyone passing through these gorges is potential prey. We don't make any exceptions."

"Then, if you have the gorges, why did you start hunting in the plains and in the city?" Jax replied.

"The Maras have been hunting in the Valley of Screams for too long," Tobiah said. "This is our turf. The daemons aren't kind or forgiving creatures. We are extremely territorial, especially where our hunting grounds are concerned. The Maras had it coming, sooner or later. Their feeding habits caused the population of large wild animals in these gorges to dwindle. There are thousands of them in that city, draining the blood from moon-bison, black deer, brown boars, and even the wolves and bears. They screwed up our raw meat sources. So we started screwing with them."

The daemon grinned, exhibiting contempt toward the Exiled Maras. This sounded like a territorial dispute between the Maras and the daemons.

"Do they know it's your people taking theirs?" I asked.

"I don't think so." Tobiah shook his head. "We usually kill those to whom we reveal ourselves. With Sienna being my obvious exception, of course... Like I said, we aren't exactly the nicest of creatures. We just had enough of the Exiled Maras killing our wild game. It was time to change the status quo, because the daemons had gotten the short end of the stick."

"And talking to them was not even on the table?" I replied, pressing my lips into a thin line.

Tobiah looked at me, then cocked his head to one side.

"How many times do I have to tell you? Daemons are not into the whole "peaceful talking and shaking hands" thing. You come to our land, you mess with our food, we hit back. So, yes, we've been hunting the citizens of Azure Heights for quite some time now. Personally, I only snatched a few, mostly from the plains. The one time I went into the city was when I saw Sienna. I haven't returned to Azure Heights since."

"So you two will just stay here, while your people kill one another?" Hansa shot back, her voice trembling with anger and her nostrils flaring. "Because once we confirm what your species does, the Exiled Maras will retaliate. It'll be a bloodbath, and it'll be thanks to *your* inability to talk things out."

Sienna moved closer to Tobiah. He put his arm around her shoulder, then dropped a kiss on the top of her head.

"I cannot intervene," the daemon replied. "I'm a free agent now, and Sienna's wellbeing is my only concern. If I get involved, my people will brand me a traitor. They won't accept any explanations or excuses. They'll just tear me to shreds, and after they're done with me, they'll eat Sienna's soul and feast on her flesh."

"We won't stand a chance," Sienna explained. "We've managed to settle here, by this pond. We may have to move later, but, for now, we're safe. But you're right about one thing. I should say something to my family, to at least give them some closure."

"That's a wise choice." Caspian nodded curtly, his jade gaze darting between her and the daemon.

"What are the chances any of you have a piece of paper and a quill, or something to write with?" Sienna looked at each of us, her eyebrows raised.

"I might be able to help," Scarlett replied, and pulled her journal and pen from her backpack, handing them over to the Exiled Mara.

Sienna then sat down on a nearby rock, scribbling a message for her brother and mother. She frequently sighed as she filled a couple of pages.

"It's difficult to find the right words," she mumbled. "I'm not sure they'll understand my relationship with Tobiah, but at least they'll know that I don't want to come back, ever again."

"You know, Vincent's somewhere nearby," I said. "He'd have come with us, but we got separated after the gorge collapsed farther back."

Sienna's head shot up, and I could see the pain in her eyes, the longing to see her brother again, before she blinked several times and returned to her initial resolve.

"I hope he's staying safe," she replied. "I don't understand why he put himself at such a risk by coming here. He barely makes it down to the first level in the city."

"He's helping us. Speaking of which, you didn't happen to see a young woman being carried around by a daemon tonight, did you?" I figured it was worth a shot, but both Sienna and Tobiah shook their heads. I sighed, disappointment weighing on me. "Okay... Back to your brother: if we give him this message for you, how will he know it's yours?"

"He should be able to recognize my handwriting, and I'll leave a special line for my brother, so he can authenticate the message as mine. We made up our own limericks when we were children." She gave me a weak smile.

I glanced ahead while she finished the message, my eyes fixing on the tracking spell under two hundred yards away. At least it was still constant on its path. Sienna and Tobiah hadn't seen Fiona around here, but that didn't mean she hadn't come this way. Maybe the daemon who took her kept her hidden.

The tracking spell was supposed to be precise, following the exact path that Fiona had taken. Sooner or later, we were going to find her. I was aiming for sooner.

18

FIONA

(DAUGHTER OF BENEDICT & YELENA)

My muscles were fully active now, but I kept myself lying on my right side, feigning weakness. Good acting was my key to getting out of this place.

Zane was lounging again by the turquoise pond, contemplating the cave's walls and many dark corners. His red eyes occasionally settled on me, his expression firm and unreadable. I really wasn't sure why he was taking so long to decide what to do with me. But, whatever the reason, I wasn't about to complain.

The sound of feet shuffling outside made my gaze dart toward the entrance. Could it be an animal, or another daemon? I sharpened my ears, hoping to pick up more. I didn't move or say anything, but Zane had heard it too. He jolted to a sitting position, staring to his right, toward the source of the sound, then glanced at me. His nostrils flared. He didn't look happy.

"Keep your mouth shut," he said under his breath, then grabbed his blades, stood, and rushed outside.

Several minutes passed. I listened carefully. It sounded as though his footsteps joined the ones already present by the cave opening. They were soon followed by a scuffle of sorts, then absolute silence. My heart skipped a beat as I realized that this was my chance to make a run for it.

I rolled onto my back, putting my booted feet against the iron bars facing the exit, the corner through which the daemon had dashed. I pulled two of the bars back, and felt the rough metal give under my grip. A couple of clangs followed as the rods came loose, leaving me enough room to crawl out of the cage.

I made it out of the small enclosure, grabbed my belt and knives off the floor, and quickly geared up before I moved toward the cave entrance. There was a narrow tunnel leading up to the exit. I stopped on the left side of the tunnel opening, my heart thumping and my blood rushing as I leaned forward to see what lay ahead. I could see faint morning light outside.

I pulled my hood over my head, then fastened the mask from my suit's collar and covered my mouth and nose. I found my goggles in their designated belt pocket, and was relieved to still have them, in case I needed them on my way out of the gorges.

Taking a couple of deep breaths and listening carefully to the noises drifting in from the outside, I waited for another minute. There was more shuffling and grunting; then it sounded as though whoever was there ran, and Zane followed, their steps becoming more distant with every second that passed.

I took my chance. Hurrying to the end of the tunnel, I stepped out into the gorge. The sun was far off to the east, hidden beyond the giant stone walls, and there was plenty of shade for me to take advantage of. I looked around, but there was no sign of Zane—just jagged rocks, tall trees with full, dark green crowns, and large shrubs scattered all over the gorge.

The city was somewhere to the east, and it was where I needed to go.

I glanced to my right, content with the absence of movement, then ran in the opposite direction. My feet were light as I jumped over broken stones and foot-wide cracks in the ground.

I'll be out in a jiff, guys. I'm coming!

I prayed I'd find my team soon, though I couldn't tell yet how many miles there were between my position and Azure Heights. Nevertheless, I ran fast, flashing through the Valley of Screams and hoping that none of the hostile creatures dwelling here would notice me.

Unfortunately, I wasn't that lucky. A few minutes later, I heard footsteps pounding behind me. Glancing over my shoulder, I saw the air rippling in three different spots, barely six feet from me. Three daemons.

"Crap," I muttered, and switched to a zigzag sprint, hoping it would be enough to put more distance between me and the invisible daemons. For all I knew, one of them could be Zane, and there was no way I was going to risk fighting them, in case I got more of that damn powder blown in my face.

A spine-freezing growl erupted from the cave I'd left behind, echoing through the gorge. My blood gushed through my veins, and sweat bloomed on my forehead. The daemons were already a potentially deadly problem, but whatever was coming from behind sounded even more terrifying than what I'd faced so far.

I flew over a small stream that gushed from the limestone wall to my right and carved its way toward the east in a sinuous line. One of the daemons slashed my right ankle —the sharp and searing pain quickly spread through my calf. I yelped and fell forward, landing flat on my face.

Unwilling to have my soul eaten, I sprang to my feet and nearly fell again, as I could no longer stand on my right leg. Blood was now spurting from my ripped boot. I pulled my long knives out and focused my stance on the left leg. I could still fight.

All I had to do was kill these three bastards, then keep going. My leg would naturally heal on its own in a matter of minutes. The daemons inched closer, surrounding me.

"I know what you look like," I hissed, baring my fangs, ready to rip their throats out. Even in their invisible state, as long as I caught glimpses of their red eyes, I could make decent approximations of where their jugulars were. "There's no point in hiding anymore."

One of them chuckled, his voice low and hoarse.

"There's no point in you trying to drag this out," he said. "You smell too wonderful for your own good!"

The one that spoke then lunged at me, but I dodged his attack while bringing my right hand out to the side, and stabbed him in the eye. A second daemon rammed into me from the left, and knocked the air out of my lungs as he kicked me down.

I landed on my back, coughing and wheezing. I slashed at the air in front of me, but they were too fast and slippery for this angle. My wrists erupted in pain as the invisible daemons hit the knives out of my hands. My arms were then pulled back over my head, while another daemon pinned my feet to the ground. Two of them were struggling to hold me down, while the third saddled my stomach and pressed his hand against my forehead.

His skin felt hot against mine, while my blood froze in response. My mouth opened, and it felt like my insides were being pulled out, inch by inch.

The pain as the daemon proceeded to chomp on my soul was unfathomable. I could see tiny wisps of white light being sucked out of my mouth, and I could feel my entire body rippling with pain.

Is this it?

I'd never experienced such levels of agony before.

I tried to scream, but my voice was tangled in my throat. The daemon pressed into my chest, cutting my breath off.

My brain burned and felt like it was about to liquefy, while my heart stammered and struggled to keep up.

Don't let this be the end...

The will to live began to dissipate like mist on an autumn morning, muted by what seemed like irreparable damage to the very fabric of my being.

I wanted to hit back. I wanted to break free and crush these beasts' heads together. I wanted to run and breathe. Even my bones hurt—a peculiar, throbbing sensation that projected outward.

My life was slowly being drained out of me. It was torture.

Suddenly, the daemon feeding off me got slammed aside, and the consumption of my soul screeched to a halt. The little flickers of white left hovering over my lips went back inside, and I coughed, breathing for the first time in what felt like forever.

Zane appeared above me for a split second, his red eyes blazing with anger. I saw flickers of his blades swishing overhead and behind him. Crimson blood sprayed out of the invisible daemons' throats. They collapsed with heavy thuds, while I finally regained control over my arms and legs.

I heard a grunt, the swoosh of Zane's blade, and a squeal, before the third daemon hit the ground.

My throat and my chest burned. My head felt heavy, and my limbs were made of lead. Sure, I could move them again, but my muscles didn't respond. Lava seemed to pour through my veins, and I groaned from the excruciating pain.

"Fiona," Zane gasped, kneeling next to me. Tears streamed down my cheeks, and my teeth clattered. I suddenly felt cold and empty beyond repair. "Fiona, look at me."

His voice was low and soothing, and it didn't match the blazing rage in his red eyes.

"And now we both look like fools," he muttered. "I underestimated your strength and you underestimated the gorge."

I shuddered, unable to control myself as I cried. I let it all out, a heart-wrenching mixture of sadness, pain, and hopelessness, all symptoms of chunks of my soul being literally eaten by daemons. I no longer had a say in how I reacted, in how I looked at the world. Not even in how I felt.

"You need to listen to me from now on, if you want to get out of here alive. Do you understand me?" he asked with a frown.

I managed a nod. He scooped me off the ground and took me in his arms. I was soft like a blob against his hard chest, his fingers digging into my flesh as he held me close and ran back toward his cave.

"You should've stayed in your cage, you stupid girl." His voice sounded farther away, though I could see him clearly. His face was mere inches from mine.

My head fell back, my neck no longer able to support its weight. Pain seared through my body, still, to the point where I feared I'd either go numb or into shock.

My eyes hurt as they rolled back, and Zane tried not to jostle me too much.

I blacked out, relieved to escape consciousness and the torment of my chewed-up soul.

19

HARPER

(DAUGHTER OF HAZEL & TEJUS)

J ax and Hansa kept asking Tobiah and Sienna questions about the daemons. Avril pulled a map of the gorges out of her backpack, for Tobiah to show us the best routes out of the Valley of Screams, and compare notes, so to speak.

The daemon obliged and gave us a brief rundown of which parts of this particular gorge were the most dangerous. We were six miles away from the western border, which opened out to wild lands inhabited by Imen tribes.

"What do *you* think?" I asked Caspian in a low voice. "Do you believe them?"

He gave me a sideways glance, his left eyebrow raised.

"Do you remember what I told you earlier tonight?" He

replied with another question, prompting me to take a deep breath and stifle an eye roll.

"'Trust no one'." I mockingly imitated his grave tone, then frowned. I looked at Tobiah and Sienna, who were currently engaged in showing Jax and Hansa potential areas where Fiona might be, based on the daemons' hunting patterns and Tobiah's knowledge of the caves. "What can we do, then?"

The couple seemed genuine, but, as Caspian had suggested, we had to be mindful of whom we trusted, regardless of their apparently innocent intentions.

"Keep following your leads, but pay attention to your instincts, as well," he replied. "For instance, what is your instinct telling you about Sienna and Tobiah?"

I took in the Exiled Mara and the daemon's expressions, looking for signs of deceit or nervous tics of any kind, but nothing grabbed my attention. There was Tobiah's discomfort at the sight of our weapons, and clear wariness toward Blaze, from both him and Sienna. Whenever the fire dragon took a step closer, their shoulders tensed.

Looking at it from their point of view, I probably would've been just as uncomfortable in the presence of a dragon that had the ability to turn me into ashes in a matter of seconds.

"They seem genuine," I murmured. "But I have my doubts, as I cannot corroborate their stories in any way. I only have their word to go on. Nevertheless, they're our only source of information right now, since you're so hellbent on keeping your mouth shut and my entire team in the dark."

Caspian scoffed and opened his mouth to say something in return, but Patrik joined us, his brow furrowed and his hands behind his back.

"What would *you* do, Lord Kifo?" Patrik asked. He'd heard us talk just now, and was most likely looking for some input. It was a smart question to ask, I thought to myself, since Caspian had been unresponsive to previous probes. "If you were in our shoes, if you were a member of GASP tasked with helping the Exiled Maras and getting one of your agents back from the daemons' claws, what would be your next move?"

"If I were in charge of this team, I'd drag you all back to Calliope and cut my losses," Caspian retorted, pursing his lips. "But clearly, that's not going to happen. Even *I* can understand that now, given how stubborn you all are. Hence, your best option is to leave Sienna and Tobiah behind and keep following that sluggish tracking spell until it leads you to Fiona. You can notify House Roho of Sienna's fate once you return to Azure Heights. If what Tobiah says is true, then you don't want to draw any daemons out here to hurt him and Sienna. They're trying to live in peace here, away from the madness and savagery of both their worlds. After all, Sienna's fine and happy, and you have your missing vampire to worry about."

The tracking spell glowed about three hundred yards away. I could still see it from here.

"I agree," Jax chimed in, his conversation with Tobiah and Sienna finished. "It's best to leave these two behind and let Vincent know when we see him. Speaking of which, any sign of the rest of our group yet, Harper?"

I used my True Sight to scan our surroundings, but I didn't see Vincent or the Correction Officers anywhere. I shook my head in response. Sienna handed me the note for her brother, folded into a small square, which I shoved in my back pocket.

"Thank you." Sienna nodded and gave us a weak smile, moving back to Tobiah's side. "I hope my brother will stop looking for me once he reads that message. I wouldn't want him to get hurt or worse by coming out here in search of me."

"You two should find a better place to live, though." Hansa gazed around with a mild frown. "This may be beautiful, but it's no home with all the daemons lurking around."

"Okay, time to go," Jax announced, then looked at Sienna and Tobiah and shrugged. "Stay out of sight, I guess. And I genuinely hope we don't cross paths again. This world is already far more complicated than we anticipated."

Sienna gave him a sheepish smile, while Tobiah frowned and offered a brief nod.

We got back on our horses. Hansa and Jax's led the way, while Scarlett and Patrik, Blaze and Caia, and Avril and

Heron followed. I climbed into the saddle, my muscles suddenly tensing as Caspian resumed his place behind me, with one arm firmly locked around my waist.

Sienna and Tobiah watched us for a minute or so, before they disappeared inside one of the crevices. The sun was rising slowly over the Valley of Screams, but we had enough shade in that gorge to not be worried about wearing goggles just yet. We only kept our hoods on as our horses galloped through the ravine, and caught up with the tracking spell.

I kept my senses alert. I listened to every sound. I caught every scent in the air. I continuously scanned the area, both behind and ahead. And I occasionally glanced over my shoulder and found Caspian watching me, his jade eyes unyielding and unwilling to betray any emotion.

I wondered if sentries could achieve mind-melds with Maras. We couldn't read their emotions, nor could we control their minds. But would I be able to join my soul with one? It wasn't an impossible premise. I'd already learned that I could syphon off a Mara.

What am I thinking?

I'd told Caspian earlier that mind-melding was a very intimate thing for us sentries. It was something my parents had accomplished after they got together. And now *I* was thinking about it, while feeling his breath on my neck.

I shook my head, mentally slapping the thought out of my brain.

20

FIONA

(DAUGHTER OF BENEDICT & YELENA)

I felt warm and cozy, despite the throbbing pain rippling through my body and clutching at my chest. I also felt drained and weak. The darkness gave me comfort. I found temporary relief in the sound of wood crackling in a fire and the murmur of water nearby.

My eyes peeled open. I blinked a couple of times, adjusting to the dim orange light flickering on the left. I was wrapped up in soft furs, and I could see knees bent on either side of me, along with a pair of strong arms locked around my torso.

I was being held close by someone. I felt the hard muscles of his chest and abs molded against my back. The memory of what had happened made *my* muscles stiffen. I tried to move, but the body keeping me there, by the fire, didn't budge.

"Don't move." Zane's gruff voice rumbled in my ear.

I stilled, my gaze darting around, as I realized where I was. I'd been brought back to the cave, after the daemons had consumed parts of my soul.

That's what this pain is...

"Drink this," he said, bringing a stone bowl to my lips. "It'll help."

There was blood in the bowl, a dark shade of crimson. Its aroma filled my lungs with the promise of healing, a rich body with underlayers of various spices that reminded me of the blood I'd had at the Spring Ball—only this was headier. He pushed the dish against my lips.

I gulped it all down, and I felt it settle in my stomach before it spread out in marvelous heatwaves that relaxed my muscles and muted the pain in my chest and limbs. I moaned softly, relief washing over me. I could finally breathe without feeling a thousand knives piercing my heart.

I melted against the furs, though my mind was already processing other potential escape methods. My body and my tattered soul were at odds with each other. My instincts told me to run, but the holes that had been burned through my existence upon the consumption of my soul were still closing.

Whatever was in that blood, it soothed me.

I'll worry about getting out of here in a minute or two.

"It tastes different," I mumbled, the back of my head resting on Zane's chest.

I should be screaming and flailing and gouging his eyes out.

"Define 'different'," he replied quietly, his chin resting on my forehead, while his hands massaged my wrists. Had I not been this daemon's prisoner, I could've sworn I was being pampered in a Nerakian spa. It felt weird, but eerily good. I knew it was just momentary relief.

I'll scream and flail and stab his eyes later. This feels good.

"It's full and rich... like coffee... but a little sweet and spicy. It's... different," I managed, my eyes half-closed as I further relaxed in his grip and enjoyed the tranquilizing effect of the blood on my now-muted inner pain.

I wiggled my feet, sensing that my ankle had already healed.

"I worried about that ankle at first," he said, as he'd felt me move, "but then I saw the wound close by itself and figured you vampires heal just like the Maras. That's a good trait to have."

"My soul," I sighed, feeling better, closer to complete with each passing minute.

"Yes, you had slivers of your soul eaten by one of those daemons," Zane replied, and I sensed the angry tremor in his voice. "Lucky for you, I tracked your scent and found you before they could finish the job. Stupid girl, you nearly got yourself killed, and trust me, having your soul devoured is not a good way to die."

"I believe you," I groaned, trying to move again, but his arms tightened around me. "I think I know what *that* feels like... And you... You saved me."

He did. He saved me. He slit the daemons' throats and brought me back here...

"I told you not to move yet," he growled. "You're still weak; you are literally missing pieces of your soul. But there's hope for you. Partial consumption is rarely permanent, especially since in your case they barely got anything before I killed them. It would take a long time for your soul to heal on its own, though, which is why I gave you that blood to drink. It's daemon blood. My blood."

I nodded, then swallowed as the actual fact sank in.

I'd just drunk Zane's blood.

"Is that why it feels so... strange?" I asked, trying to analyze all the reactions that my body displayed under his influence.

"Yes," he replied. "Daemons digest souls the same way in which they digest regular food. It gets absorbed into our bloodstream. It's pure energy, and souls react to each other. Once my blood enters your stream, the soul particles it contains simply spread out and fill the gaps in your being."

"I think they're already doing that..."

"Good. It means your soul is reacting positively to my blood. You silly, lucky girl." He scoffed.

While it did feel odd to accept that someone's soul was flowing through me, I also relished the soothing effect of his unconventional treatment. I then figured it was as good a time as any to try to ask some questions. After all, an injury had never stopped me from gathering intel before—and it wouldn't now, even when I was lying in the arms of a daemon, with a tattered soul. I tilted my head to see his face, and found him watching me intently, the fire next to us reflected in his red eyes.

"Why did you help me? Why didn't you just let me die? What do the daemons want?" I asked, my voice still weak.

A handful of seconds went by as he said nothing, then smirked.

"You still don't understand, do you?" he replied. "You're in over your head, Fiona. You shouldn't ask questions. You won't like the answers."

"I'm just trying to understand your motivation." I shrugged. "You seem different from the other daemons."

"That is a dangerous assumption to make, little vampire."

"I don't think so. After all, I'm still here. In fact, you stopped your fellow daemons from eating my soul, and you've even given me your own blood to help me heal."

He held my gaze for a while, then looked at the fire crackling next to us. His shoulders dropped, but his grip on me was firm.

"Honestly, I don't know what I'm doing, either." He

sighed. I tried not to smile, counting this as a minor victory. "Your soul smells so damn good. Every fiber in my body is telling me to consume you, to take it all and kill you. But you're a strange creature, and I can't figure you out. Maybe after I understand what makes you tick, I *will* eat your soul, then rip your chest open and feast on your still-beating heart, too."

A chill traveled down my spine. My instincts were coming back to me. My defenses were gradually building themselves back up, and he felt my body tense. His eyes found mine, and I noticed a muscle twitching in his jaw.

"There were so many daemons in the prison last night," he muttered. "They'd all caught your scent. They all wanted a piece of you. But I wanted you the most, and I do *not* share my food with anyone."

The recent memory of Zane sharing his wild boar with me came to mind, a direct contradiction to what he'd just said.

"Why were you all in the prison last night? Did the Maras let you in?" I asked.

He didn't answer, but he narrowed his eyes. His face inched closer to mine. I held my breath, racking my brain for another way out of this predicament. I had a feeling my comfort was only temporary.

"What do you intend to do with me? You mentioned me getting out of here," I added, my gaze wandering to the tips of his ivory horns.

He pulled his head back, cocking it to one side, his expression moody.

"I won't eat your soul. For now," he replied bluntly. "But I might change my mind and come after you later."

More chills trickled down my spine, my nerves stretching in response to the prospect of having my soul eaten and experiencing that torturous agony again. I shuddered, and he felt it. The corner of his mouth twitched as he tightened his arms around me, as if trying to reassure me that he'd said he *might* come after me later, not that he *would*.

Yeah, not making me feel better...

"I can't keep you here forever, either," he continued nonchalantly. "There are too many daemons around, and I can't waste my time making sure you don't escape again. Besides, I still have work in the area, and babysitting you would be a nuisance."

My teeth were grinding as I tried to skip past the "babysitting" part.

"What work is that?" I asked.

"I thought I told you not to ask questions. You won't like the answers." He smirked.

"Life isn't always about getting what we like, anyway," I retorted. "I need some truth here. You can't keep me in the dark."

"Of course, you won't make this any easier, will you?"

I opened my mouth to object, but he brought his hand

up to my face. I caught a glimpse of an orange powder in his palm. I didn't get a chance to react before he blew it in my face.

I wheezed and coughed, then completely mellowed in his arms. My muscles were mush. Whatever that powder was, it was more powerful than the red one. It nearly paralyzed me, turning me into a ragdoll.

Zane hauled me up, then threw me over his shoulder. I groaned but couldn't formulate clear sentences. The orange powder had disabled my speech, too. I was putty in his hands, and I couldn't even speak.

I hate you.

"Time to take you back to your tribe," he said, then pulled the hood over my head, grabbed my belt with knives off the ground, and sauntered out of the cave.

"Wha... Why..." I managed as he carried me through the gorge.

I couldn't even look up. My neck muscles were too weak. But the gorge was still shaded, the sun still lazily rising in the east.

"My scouts saw your people five miles east of here," he explained. I got a good view of his naked back and the pebbled ground he walked on. My cheeks caught fire as I found myself staring at his glutes moving beneath his loincloth, and the smooth lines of his tanned calves.

"I... talk..." I tried, but my tongue worked like a lump of stone. As in, it didn't.

He chuckled lightly, his left arm tight around my thighs, while my arms hung limply over his back.

"Yeah, I toned you down a little too much, didn't I?" He sounded amused. "I just wanted to enjoy a little peace and quiet with you, without all your questions and silly bravado."

I hate you.

"Worry not, little vampire," he added. "You'll be back with your friends soon enough. As much as I'd like it, keeping you around is a bit of a logistical nightmare. They brought the dragon out, and if they go any deeper, the whole gorge will blow up. It's best if I bring you to them now; it's too early in the morning for such unnecessary hostilities."

That explanation definitely made me feel better. I was being taken back to GASP, who I now knew for a fact were somewhere in the gorge, looking for me, and Blaze was with them. Hope blossomed in my chest, while Zane's blood continued to fix the damage that the daemons had done to my soul.

At the same time, however, I was dismayed. I'd gotten a glimpse of a daemon's hunting grounds, sure. I'd learned a couple of minor things about the species. But other than that, I had nothing to bring back to my team, other than myself with my ass handed to me.

21

AVRIL

(DAUGHTER OF LUCAS & MARION)

S everal hours passed uneventfully, and I didn't know whether to feel relieved or worried. The gorge became awfully quiet again as we rode our horses through it, heading farther west, after the tracking spell. The light orb was still constant and slow, and my stomach churned with concern over Fiona's wellbeing.

The sun had already passed over us, and the noon heat actually felt good through my leather suit. We had our hoods, masks, and goggles on, as there was enough sunshine to give us serious burns if we were to expose ourselves to it.

Our indigo horses were also quiet, their tails flicking occasionally as we advanced along the freshwater stream. I glanced over my shoulder and stifled a smirk, watching

Harper, who shared a horse with Caspian. They barely spoke, while Harper looked particularly stiff with his arm wrapped around her waist.

I then shifted my focus to Heron, who stared ahead and spoke even fewer words since we'd left Sienna and Tobiah behind. Jax and Hansa were talking to Caia and Blaze, their horses leading our group, while Scarlett and Patrik shared observations about the ravine's flora and fauna.

Harper scanned the area every twenty minutes or so, looking for Vincent and the Correction Officers in neighboring gorges, but came up with nothing every time. They'd either gotten lost or killed.

Or worse, they left us here to die.

I shook the ominous thought away, then went over our brief conversation with Sienna and Tobiah. Based on her account and what we'd learned from Arrah and the other Imen servants at the Roho mansion, certain pieces were starting to fit into the puzzle, while most remained obscure.

The daemons were true to their hunting pattern, after all. They'd kept to the Valley of Screams for a long time, until they grew fed up with the Exiled Maras grabbing all the big game. So they started hunting more Exiled Maras and Imen instead, gradually breaching the plain, then working their way into Azure Heights.

They were invisible when hunting, as per Bear and Sinon's information—the two rogue Imen we'd encountered during our mission to stuff charmed satchels into the moun-

tain base for Patrik's protection spell. They were ridiculously fast and vicious, their hits aiming to kill. They were
territorial creatures that lived underground—and I was
getting curious as to what their life looked like beneath the
surface of Neraka. Given their appearance and behavior, I
could only assume that they were warriors, crude and
vengeful. Tobiah had also confirmed that repeatedly:
daemons were not nice creatures.

At the same time, there was something off in Azure
Heights. The Maras were strict about their laws, and too
secretive about their prison. There were plenty of mysteries
left to untangle down there—despite what the warden had
said, I had a hard time chalking the gate incident up to a
technical glitch. The prisoners were in a poor state, and I
looked forward to investigating further. Something in the
back of my head kept telling me there was a clear connection between Arrah and that place, and that it all boiled
down to Demios and the validity of the charges against him.

We knew that Arrah's brother could be used as leverage
against the young Iman girl, who was an enigma all by
herself—impervious to a Mara's mind-bending, and
seeming to possess more knowledge about the prison and
the daemons than she let on. While Sienna had been an
anomaly in the abduction pattern, we did know why:
Tobiah had first seen her on the first level, where the
hunting actually took place; he'd fallen for her, and he'd
followed her around before snatching her. Did Arrah know

all that, or was there something else that had pushed either House Kifo or Roho (or both, for that matter) to incarcerate Demios and force her into silence?

I then remembered Cynara, the servant girl we'd met during our first night on Neraka. We'd yet to speak to her and her sister, Hera, after we'd seen Cynara get carried out of the dining room at the Broken Bow Inn. I made a mental note to follow up on that lead once we got back to Azure Heights. Maybe she knew something.

I was also suspicious about mind-bending. The Exiled Maras had been adamant about their motivations: they'd used their abilities on the Imen to force the truth out of suspected criminals, and to help the families of abductees cope with their losses. Nevertheless, one too many of the Imen in the city had displayed symptoms of mind-bending. Another thing that added to my concerns regarding the wellbeing of the Imen focused on their seemingly short life spans, and that illness we'd learned about back at the Roho mansion.

The slumber before death...

"What are you thinking about?" Heron asked, breaking my inner process.

"Everything." I shrugged.

He pulled his goggles down, his jade eyes piercing through my soul. Our mission on Neraka had been so weird and so confusing that I'd barely had enough time to properly monitor my reactions to Heron's presence. Our brief exchanges had lodged a bothersome rock into the wheels of our friendship, as we were slowly gravitating toward each other. I feared that if we got closer, we'd both explode.

"The tracking spell is picking up speed, though it's just an extra mile per hour," he said, nodding toward the light orb ahead.

I glanced at it for a moment, and realized he was right. We were moving a little faster. My gears kicked into motion, my heartrate spiking. I gave him a half-smile.

"We're getting closer," I confirmed.

"We'll get her back, Avril," he reassured me with a mild frown.

"I know." I nodded, and couldn't help but wonder what he was thinking in that moment. Most of his face was concealed by his mask. I only had his pale green gaze to work with.

Noises ahead made us break eye contact. Caspian and Harper's horse trotted forward, passing us and slowing down by Jax and Hansa's side.

The gorge walls were widening again. Tall trees lined both sides, their rich crowns spreading outward and concealing most of the blue sky above. They reminded me of the redwoods back home, towering over the world and making everything look puny by comparison. Large slabs of limestone and voluminous ferns and shrubs were scattered along the walls, most of them concealing grottos and smaller crevices.

The stream flowed through the middle of the space ahead, before the walls drew closer together again. And there was a mass of... creatures moving toward us in an organized fashion, about two hundred yards away.

"Get out of sight. Now!" Caspian whispered.

We immediately pulled our horses to the side and got off just after the gorge widened. Harper used her mind control on the animals, her eyes glimmering as her hands gripped the sword handles strapped to her belt. She directed the horses behind a cluster of jagged rocks.

"Stay here. Do not move," she commanded.

We followed Caspian, sneaking along the righthand side behind tall chunks of stone and between the trees, getting closer to the small crowd. We found cover behind a towering rock, fifty feet from the strange group. I held my breath as I got a better look.

There were about sixty Imen huddled into four large iron cages mounted on wheels, each mobile enclosure being pulled by a giant beast roughly the size of an elephant. The creatures looked like a cross between a bear and a wolf, with no fur and ink-black skin. Their backs and legs were stocked with bulging muscles. Their eyes shone red, and they had huge fangs and claws to go with the whole ensemble. They were downright frightening fiends, as if someone had decided to engineer the hounds of hell, but on steroids. The beasts had massive black iron collars tightened around their robust necks, with several symbols painted in red.

"That's swamp witch magic," Patrik muttered, consternation smoothing his forehead and widening his blue eyes.

That wasn't the worst part, though. The cages were also guarded by at least four dozen daemons, visible, clad in heavy armor, and carrying spears and rapiers. They were different from the others we'd seen before. They were organized and disciplined, covered in protective gear and wielding weapons.

Just when I'd thought I'd learned enough about the daemons and their customs, more questions popped up like mushrooms after the rain. I couldn't help but voice them in a whispering avalanche:

"Where'd they get the swamp witch magic? Did they steal knowledge from the Exiled Maras, or was it willingly given to them? What the heck are those gargantuan beasts? What purpose do the collars serve? Where are they taking all those Imen?"

"I suggest you save those questions for later," Caspian breathed, crouching in front of us. "If you want to survive, that is."

"Fine, but do you at least know what those oversized creatures are?" Harper retorted, gritting her teeth.

"Pit wolves," Caspian replied, keeping his voice low. "They're rare but deadly. They're faster than Maras and most likely faster than you, too. They'll sniff us out if we keep following them, so stay put. Let them go ahead."

My stomach twisted itself into painful knots as I

watched our tracking spell quietly hover above the crowd, without moving forward.

"What's up with the tracking spell?" I murmured, and Patrik craned his neck, frowning.

"I... I have no idea," he whispered.

"What do we do?" I asked, looking at Hansa and Jax, whose frowns didn't make me feel any better. Heron was next to me, while Scarlett stayed behind Patrik. We turned away from the crowd and huddled closer together, our backs against the rock as we faced the redwoods and limestone walls.

"Those are Imen from western tribes beyond the gorge," Caspian said slowly. "They were most likely captured during a daemon raid."

"Daemon raids? Are you freaking serious?" Harper was outraged. I couldn't blame her. Fire and ice burst through me as I imagined an organized attack on an unsuspecting village, and innocent Imen dragged from their homes and shoved into cages.

"Yes, Miss Hellswan, I'm serious," Caspian shot back, obviously irritated. By the looks of him, he *really* didn't want us to be here. I figured this convoy took him by surprise. "The daemons don't just hunt in the gorges. They're an organized society, as you can see for yourself by the cages, the armor, and the weapons."

"Where are they taking them? They're headed east

through the gorge, and I doubt they're delivering them to Azure Heights." Hansa huffed.

"There's probably a route through these parts that leads underground into their cities," Caspian replied.

Cities. The daemons have underground cities.

Harper had been right all along. Caspian definitely knew a lot more than he was letting on.

"What. Do. We. Do?" I asked again.

"Do we fight them? I mean, you still have me." Blaze shrugged, removing his eye bandage. He was completely healed, the muscles on his bare chest and shoulders twitching with anticipation. He was itching for a fight.

"We need to get to Fiona." Jax frowned, pressing his lips into a tight, frustrated line before he cursed under his breath.

"But the tracking spell is still. And it's only a matter of time before they notice it," I murmured. I could feel my nerves snapping, one by one, as I listened to the iron wheels screeching and turning, the cages behind us being pulled through the gorge. I heard the pit wolves' grunting. The daemons' footsteps on the hard ground. The yelps and moans of the captive Imen. The poor creatures knew that they were being led to their deaths.

What could we do? The pit wolves alone could represent a challenge, along with fifty or more daemons in full armor and with plenty of blades between them. They carried shields, too. These weren't the brazen hunters we'd dealt with earlier—even those had been quick and smart enough to poke Blaze in the eye and nearly disable him mid-fight.

If we were to let Blaze loose in dragon form, we would have to drag the Imen out of the way for him to let his devastating fires loose. Otherwise we'd end up tiptoeing around their cages with a lizard the size of a passenger plane, and, in the meantime, Fiona's tracking spell could dart away after her before any of us even saw it.

We may be a tad screwed...

22

HARPER

(DAUGHTER OF HAZEL & TEJUS)

"I strongly recommend that we all stay put and wait for the convoy to pass," Caspian whispered. "Some, if not all of you, might get killed if you try anything against these beasts."

"Some of *you*? Not including yourself in that statement?" I raised an eyebrow.

He gave me an acid smirk.

I could smack him. I could totally smack him.

"I'm not suicidal. I'm only trying to help," he replied. "You can't get yourselves tangled in another fight now, even if you do have a dragon. You need to get to Fiona and get the hell out of these gorges before you all end up as pit wolf chow."

"I hate to say this, I really do," Hansa sighed, her brow

furrowed, "but Lord Kifo has a point."

No, don't say that. He'll give me a smug smile, and... There it is.

Caspian loved being right, apparently.

"There are plenty of them, and those giant fiends are something else entirely," Hansa continued. "We *have* to get to Fiona before it's too late, and we can then gather more forces from Calliope and tear these gorges down altogether, and—"

A bone-chilling growl, like chunks of glass being scraped against a pavement, came from above. We all froze, then glanced up and noticed the elephant-sized pit wolf baring its enormous white fangs at us. Its red eyes glistened with hunger; thick threads of drool hung from its lower jaw.

"Crap," I heard Jax say.

We jumped back, drawing our swords. My heart nudged into my throat, and my blades were soon up and ready. It was too late to debate this further. We hadn't even seen or heard the beast move.

Our only choice was to fight.

"Stand back," Blaze said as the pit wolf growled and wiggled its hindquarters, ready to pounce on us.

We scattered to both sides as Blaze erupted into full dragon form. He knocked over a couple of redwoods. I dodged one of the massive trees, which landed heavily to my right.

The daemons went on high alert, raising their swords

and spears. Half of them charged us, while one of the fiends left behind set the other pit wolves loose. The rest guarded the cages, which came to a screeching halt. The Imen inside gathered in the middle, crying and trying their best to cover each other from whatever came next.

We spread out and darted toward the first wave of daemons coming. Caia ignited her lighters and fashioned two impressively thick fire whips, which she used to lash at one of the pit wolves, while Patrik muttered a spell under his breath and summoned a spray of intense blue fire from his hands, aiming it at the armored daemons.

Their protective gear made it more difficult for us to kill them but not impossible, as evidenced by Hansa's broadsword chopping a couple of heads down like she was an expert lumberjack. In the absence of mind-bending as a useful weapon against the daemons, Heron and Jax made full use of their blades, flashing from one daemon to another. Their blows were swift and heavy, drawing spurts of crimson blood as they tackled multiple opponents at once, dodging hits and veering left and right between them.

Blaze tackled another pit wolf, snapping his fangs at it between brief sessions of clawing and spiking daemons. His tail was most effective in this part of the gorge, flailing and lashing around with deadly precision. Soon enough, bodies started to drop, most of them mangled and torn into pieces.

Avril was handling her fair share of daemons, while Scarlett used her stunning speed to confuse a second pit wolf, slashing its limbs whenever she managed to get close. Caspian was right—these oversized dogs *were* faster than the average Mara or vampire. Luckily for us, so was Scarlett.

Speaking of the jade-eyed devil, Caspian stayed close to my side as we fought incoming daemons. I was extremely energized, with an extra kick in my step I instantly attributed to Caspian—I could feel his power burning through me, rivers of bright green fire igniting my reflexes as I swerved to the left and ran my sword through the narrow space between two metal plates mounted on a daemon's torso. I drew blood. The fiend hissed from the pain but didn't get his chance to strike back. I turned and stabbed him in the neck, both blades protruding beneath his chin.

"Harper, watch out!" I heard Caspian say.

I heard shuffling behind me and jolted out of the way, just as a spear missed my hip by an inch. I charged the daemon, bringing both swords down in a flurry of repetitive hits. My foot went out to the side, kicking his left knee hard enough to make him falter in his defense. It was all I needed to bring one sword across and cut his shield arm off in one move. I swiftly followed it with a 360-degree twist, both blades extended to separate his head from his neck. Blood sprayed out. I caught a glimpse of Caspian fighting two daemons at once.

Blaze growled as he continued to plow through the first wave of daemons, until two pit wolves tried to sink their teeth into his muscular thighs. He managed to catch one in his jaws, crunching and chewing. The beast squealed and eventually stopped moving. The other yelped and scampered to the side, looking for another attack angle, while Blaze spit his partner out and proceeded to launch his calculated attacks against other daemons.

Two more were coming at me, but I didn't get a chance to fight them. A sharp pain pierced through my stomach, and I stilled, unable to breathe. I saw Caspian freeze, his mask torn off and horror imprinted on his face. I glanced down and gasped at the sight of a blade poking from my abdomen, of blood flowing out of me and pooling at my feet.

My knees grew weak as I realized we had more company. Invisible hunters had joined the fight, and one of them had just stabbed me with a long knife. The pain spread out through my torso, and I felt warm blood rising in my throat. This wasn't going to kill me, but whatever came next most definitely could.

I tried to move, but all I managed to do was cough up some blood before the daemon kicked me in the back. He didn't stand a chance, though, as Caspian slashed his opponents down in a fit of rage and lunged at the invisible fiend behind me. The daemon kicked me again, trying to set his arm free. I fell flat on my face, my entire body shuddering and breaking into a cold sweat, the pain too strong to let me stand up or even push myself off the ground.

Caspian's roar made my muscles tighten. He rammed his sword through the invisible daemon's eyes. He then scooped me up in his arms and carried me away from the hot zone, hiding us behind a redwood. He put me down, my back leaning against a stone. I struggled to keep a steady breath, the pain searing through my torso.

"You'll be okay," he breathed, then bit into his wrist and pushed it against my lips. "Drink!"

I nodded and let his blood fill my mouth. I suckled at his wrist with greed, feeling my insides burn as they healed surprisingly fast. His jade eyes were clouded. He chewed on his lower lip, occasionally glancing down at my wound.

The pain subsided as I drank more of Caspian's blood, and I nearly choked when I started seeing ribbons of color flowing out of him. I could feel my gaping wound close, the muscles and tendons repairing themselves. The battle raged on behind us.

I could *feel* him. I could feel his emotions tickling my senses, a mixture of pitch-black anger and bright blue hope, thoroughly intertwined with something warm and gold, a feeling I wasn't sure how to label. His gaze softened as he withdrew his wrist and wiped the blood from my lips with his thumb.

It turned out I finally had an open channel to Caspian's emotions. And his blood had facilitated that.

Hah... Gotcha now...

My spine tingled as he leaned closer, his nose brushing

gently against mine and his expression soft. His breath warmed my lips.

"Don't scare me like that again, Miss Hellswan," he whispered, the green pools in his eyes darkening. "I didn't come all the way here to watch you die."

He slipped his arms around my torso and helped me up. I leaned into him, comfortable against his firm chest, and looked up.

"Thank you," I sighed, once again revitalized and eager to get back into the action behind me.

He was the first Mara I could read, and I tried very hard to stifle my satisfaction, feeling it spread all over my face with a wide grin. He frowned.

"What's so funny?" he asked.

"Nothing." I cleared my throat and pushed myself away, pleased to be able to stand on my own again. "Just... Thank you..."

Caspian nodded, then quickly scanned the battlefield.

"Your swords are back there," he noted, then put his hands on my shoulders. "Ready to go back in?"

I glanced over my shoulder and saw Patrik drawing water from the nearby stream to reveal the dozens of invisible daemons that had invaded this part of the gorge. There were fewer than twenty armored daemons left, but at least five dozen hunters as backup and three remaining pit wolves.

The rest of my team was holding its own while the

Druid tried to reveal as many invisible daemons as possible. Judging by the way the air rippled across the battlefield, they were strategically scattered, as if they'd already figured out Patrik's range.

"Yeah, I'm ready," I said.

I darted out and went straight for my knives. Two daemons obstructed my path. I drew my long knives out as I slid down onto my back and slipped between one daemon's legs, slashing the insides of his thighs before I reached for my swords.

I sheathed the knives and grabbed my twin blades, then jumped to my feet.

Caspian threw me a casual wink and a smile as he engaged another daemon. My heart fluttered in my chest, and I rode that feeling into another fight.

Three daemons snarled as they charged me from three different angles.

"Three's a party!" I grinned, and let loose.

Whatever flowed through Caspian's veins passed as blood but was loaded with delicious energy. I'd had my fill earlier, replenishing my sentry strength, but I was even more buzzed after drinking his blood. My muscles tingled as I gripped the handles on my swords and switched to an attack stance.

This was going to be good.

These bastards won't stand a chance.

23

SCARLETT

(DAUGHTER OF JERAMIAH & PIPPA)

Two of the pit wolves set their sights on me, while Blaze dealt with the third one and the armored daemons. I was fast enough to keep myself out of the mutts' jaws, though they tried to attack me from different angles. I was able to keep track of both as they darted around. I slashed at one just as it snapped its teeth at my leg, missing my calf by an inch. I drew blood and heard it squeal before it retreated to attempt another strike.

I quickly glanced around. The daemons were slowly losing to our team, with a large number of casualties attributed to Blaze. Though he was careful not to harm us or the Imen prisoners, the dragon was still agile and precise enough to deal deadly blows to entire hostile clusters. My blood chilled as I noticed the armored daemons swallow something—one by one, they shimmered, then vanished.

The realization hit me in the stomach with the weight of a sledgehammer.

"Patrik, they're using swamp magic!" I shouted. "The invisibility spell! That's what it is!"

I heard him groan and curse under his breath. He was dealing with his fair share of daemons, switching between his blade and blue-fire spells to take them down, weakening them so Avril and Heron could finish them off.

He pushed a fiery pulse out, the blue flames engulfing five daemons at once, then summoned a shower of water from the nearby stream to reveal the fiends that had just gone invisible. I counted at least fifty now, including the ten still guarding the Imen's cages.

One of the pit wolves that had been nagging me shifted its focus to Patrik, prowling behind him. The Druid was too busy with daemons to notice the beast coming up behind him. It was moving too fast for me to even warn him. My heart thudded as I flashed after it.

I slipped between Patrik and the fiend, and drove my sword upward. The blade pierced its throat. Blood gushed out and coated me in crimson. The pit wolf collapsed with a dying groan. I looked over my shoulder and registered Patrik's astonishment before he blocked hits from two daemons.

The second pit wolf that I'd dealt with was hot on my

tail. It dodged a spike hit from Blaze, then darted at me. I blocked its attacks as it repeatedly tried to claw at me. Its fiery red eyes were filled with rage. It had watched as two of its kind were brought down. It was out for blood.

Its growls sent chills down my spine, while I tried looking for a weak spot. The neck was my best bet. I faked a move to the right, enough to get the pit wolf to stretch its neck after me, then immediately flashed a couple of steps to the left. It jerked back a little too soon, so when I rammed my sword into the beast, the blade punctured the iron collar.

Crap!

Everything that came afterward happened in slow motion. Its jaws were gaping, its long fangs sharp and eager to tear me apart. I tried to pull the blade back. I tugged in order to dislodge it and wound up breaking the collar off entirely. The pit wolf stilled as the fragmented iron fell to the ground.

It shook its head, looking around with awe and confusion, as if it had just been put there. It glanced at me and yelped, its massive head lowering in a fearful gesture. Its red eyes were wide and filled with angst, and it took a couple of steps back.

I moved forward with the intention of finishing it off, but never got that chance. The pit wolf scurried off in the opposite direction and disappeared behind a string of boulders. It was baffling, to say the least. I thought about the collar symbols that Patrik had identified as swamp witch magic. Could it be that those iron bands were influencing the animals' behavior?

Only one way to find out, I thought to myself as I set my sights on the last pit wolf, which was still shuffling around Blaze, trying to get a good attack angle on him. It was moving fast, but I needed to somehow take it by surprise.

Patrik was several feet away from me, fighting three armored daemons. I took a second to admire his agility— the way he swerved around the hostiles as if he were made of water, the speed of his sword, and his excellent coordination between his sword and his Druid spells.

He dodged a rapier slash, then pushed a bright golden energy pulse out, which knocked the daemons off their feet. The fiends fell backward, grunting and panting from the impact. Patrik then threw out blue fires that engulfed the daemons. They screamed, flailing their arms and desperately rolling over the ground to put the flames out.

I jumped in and rammed my sword through one of them, the blade puncturing his throat, while Patrik swiftly finished off the other two. He looked at me, breathing heavily from what already seemed like an eternity of fighting.

"I'll tell you one thing," I gasped. "It wasn't this intense during GASP training!"

He gave me a brief, sympathetic smile before he looked to his right, as more daemons advanced toward us.

"There are still too many of them," Patrik said, resuming his attack stance, with his sword out and his right hand glowing gold and ready to deal another blow to the incoming hostiles.

"I never knew you could remove the invisibility spell using water, not until we came here and met the daemons," I replied, catching a glimpse of Caia as she pulled water out of the stream and used it to reveal daemons. She wasn't as well versed with water manipulation as she was with fire, but she could still use this part of her fae ability if she needed to.

"Technically speaking, it isn't possible," Patrik said, "but you are right. I saw them swallow something, too. The collar symbols, their ability to go invisible like this, it all points to swamp witch magic. Maybe they altered the spells."

He leaned into his left leg, ready to jump at the daemons approaching him, their spears pointing at him. I caught another glimpse of the pit wolf prowling behind Blaze's hind legs. This was my chance.

"I'm going to test a theory now," I muttered, then flashed by Patrik's side, bringing my face close to his for a split second. "Kick their asses, Patrik."

I then darted after the last pit wolf, moving around the hot zone where the team was actively fighting daemons. I dodged several hits on the way, as the hostiles did try to get me but quickly realized that I was too fast. I closed the distance between me and the pit wolf and brought my sword up, ready to make the most of the angle I was working to hit the collar. I wanted to see if, by removing the iron, the pit wolf's behavior would change. The beast used his momentum and climbed onto Blaze's thigh, moving fast to travel the length of the dragon's back and reach the eyes.

Blaze's giant head then swooped into the frame, his jaws closing with a loud crack as he snapped the pit wolf in two. He jerked it around several times, then spat it on the ground. I came to a full stop right in front of the creature's mangled body, cursing under my breath.

I looked up at Blaze and shook my head.

"Dude, I was onto it! You ruined my experiment!" I shouted.

Blaze stared at me for a couple of seconds, his midnight-blue eyes flickering black as he blinked. He then huffed and resumed his systematic attack on the incoming daemons.

"So much for figuring out whether that collar actually does something or I just freaked the pit wolf out..." I muttered, then glanced over my shoulder and raised my sword to block a daemon's attack.

He viciously clawed at the empty space that I kept putting between us, then screamed after my blade swooped down in a circular motion and cut off his hands altogether. I executed a rapid 180-degree turn with the blade out as I gripped its handle with both hands and decapitated the fiend. His head rolled at my feet, his red eyes bulging with shock as life dissipated from his features.

I looked at the Imen cages fifty yards to our left, which were still guarded by some daemons, then briefly analyzed the battlefield. If we could get the Imen out of the way and let them free, we could give Blaze the space he needed to spit fire and carbonize all the daemons at once.

I noticed Hansa and Jax were the closest, just twenty yards from one of the cages.

"Hansa, Jax!" I called out. "Set the Imen free so Blaze can burn these horned suckers down!"

"Good thinking!" Hansa replied just as she managed to ram her broadsword through a daemon's chest. She kicked the hostile off her blade, taking a step back for Jax to cut his head off.

I moved closer to their side, engaging the other daemons surrounding them in a separate fight. It gave Jax and Hansa the window they needed to run to the cages.

My body whizzed with energy and determination. We had to wrap this up sooner, rather than later, if we wanted to get to Fiona in time. Every second we wasted fighting daemons was a second we could've spent tracking Fiona. That thought alone was enough to add a dash of strength to my sword hits as I tackled multiple opponents at once.

There's no way you jerks are getting between us and Fiona any longer!

24

JAX

There were fewer than twenty yards between us and the Imen's cages, and about ten daemons left guarding them. The others had moved onto the battlefield, and half of those were already dead. Had it not been for the throng of invisible hunters that came out of nowhere, we would've finished them all off by now.

Hunters must have been in the area, maybe surveying the high points of the gorge or prowling through the crevices. One thing was clear, though: they were fierce and quick to jump in to help the other fiends. I figured they wanted to protect the Imen transport at all costs—based on what Caspian had told us, it seemed reasonable to assume that these cages were meant to feed the daemons underground, those who were unable to hunt for themselves.

Scarlett took center stage on Hansa's and my fighting

ground, fending off incoming hostiles so we could take care of the cages. Our objective was to break the locks and help the Imen escape—get them as far away from the area as possible. We could then jump behind the nearest rocks and leave Blaze with the freedom he needed to unleash his dragon fire.

One of the ten daemons in charge of the prisoners came at me, his metallic armor screeching as he raised his spear. I ducked and dodged the hit, then drove my swords through the sides of his torso, where the chest plates were joined to the rest of the protective gear with threaded mesh. It was one of the few soft spots I'd identified in the daemons' armor. The fiend collapsed to his knees. Hansa moved forward and tackled two more that had been stationed around the first cage.

We fought them hard—they were desperate and thus unpredictable. Their chaotic attacks made us burn a lot of energy swerving left and right to avoid their blades, before we could get a clear shot. Eventually, they both came down, their heads tumbling onto the hard ground, blood pooling at our feet.

The Imen were huddled in the middle, crying and trembling, crouching and covering their heads. Hansa was looking for the locks when a fourth daemon emerged from behind the cage and came at her with his rapier, the blade sharp and glistening with eagerness to slice her.

I dashed to her side and blocked the attack with my

swords, then kicked the fiend in his groin. He doubled over in pain, giving me the perfect position to chop his head off. Sure, daemons were fast and vicious, but, like all two-legged creatures I'd ever come across, some were weaker and were victims of poor choices fueled by panic.

Hansa's emerald-gold eyes brightened as she glanced at me. She gave me a brief but sincere smile, and I could feel the ice between us thawing. Our ride on the same horse had already been equal parts intense and uncomfortable. I was relieved to see her not glaring at me or completely ignoring me. The color suddenly left her cheeks, and she lunged at me, gripping her broadsword with both hands, blade aimed at my torso.

It happened so fast that I didn't even have a reaction. My heart paused as I watched her ram her sword just inches from my right side, and I heard a grunt behind me. I glanced over my shoulder and saw the air rippling, along with a pair of narrowed red eyes—this was a tall daemon, towering two feet over me.

I suddenly turned, and used the speed of that movement to pierce his neck with my sword. The fiend collapsed, his body hitting the ground and crimson blood gushing from his wounds.

"Remind me to thank you later for this," I said to Hansa, then moved around the cage. More invisible daemons rushed toward us.

"No need, just looking out for my team," Hansa

breathed, resuming her search for the locks. One of the Imen looked at her and pointed to his left. Two locks held the cage closed on that side.

She wasn't going to get a moment to reach those padlocks, as more daemons gathered around us. Caia was busy with a dozen hostiles on her side, while Blaze continued his targeted attacks. Avril and Heron helped Patrik finish off the remaining armored daemons, but more invisible hunters came in from the narrower parts of the gorge that we'd left behind. Harper and Caspian had their fair share of daemons to deal with, while Scarlett kept flashing around and pitching in on all sides, her flurry of rapid hits causing blood showers to spray around in shades of vivid crimson.

I had to give Hansa the break she needed to set the Imen free.

Two can play that game, I thought to myself as I fumbled through my belt compartments and scooped out a handful of invisibility paste. I always carried some with me, to use in situations such as this. Hansa was too busy to notice me swallowing the swamp witches' spell, and there was no time for me to explain.

I circled toward her, feeling my body buzzing, the invisibility spell kicking in. I pushed her aside as daemons crashed into me. She landed on her back and most likely saw me swallowed by a horde of invisible daemons. She screamed.

"Jax!"

Forgive me, Hansa...

The fiends couldn't see me anymore. They stilled and growled. I didn't move either, waiting to see if they'd sense my presence still there. I'd managed to confuse them for long enough to calculate exactly how I'd kill them all.

Breathe.

I exhaled sharply and cut the head off the first daemon on my right. The blood spurts drew the others' attention, and they all jumped in to tear the invisible body apart—mistaking it for mine. I avoided direct contact with the bodily fluids spewing out of the scuffle as the fiends ended up slashing and cutting each other. I flung my swords around and opened large gashes wherever my blades made contact, then backed away and watched the air trembling around the mass of invisible daemons tearing each other apart.

Hansa fought off more fiends on her side, her body glowing silver as she chopped their limbs off in a rage-fueled rampage. I managed to sneak to the cage we'd been trying to open. I put my swords away and cracked both padlocks off with a rock. The Imen mumbled and gasped as they poured out and ran toward the western part of the gorge, scattering so they wouldn't all get trapped or caught again.

I made my way to the second cage, where two armored daemons waited, while Hansa tackled an invisible hunter and shoved her broadsword right between his bright red eyes. She roared as she killed another one on her way to the third cage, just ten yards away from my position. I wanted to say something, but, again, time wasn't on my side. I took advantage of my invisibility and obliterated the two guards with four strikes, two per jugular. I heard shouting to the left, where the rest of my team was, the stream flowing behind them. I glanced in their direction and quickly assessed the scene. Invisible daemons kept pouring in, with Caia and Patrik taking turns in summoning water to splash and reveal them all.

A peculiar swish caught my eye, followed by movement from the right side. A new, foreign presence flew in, gliding over the brook. She looked like a young woman with long, pale blond—almost white—hair. She didn't seem a day over twenty, and was petite, with her upper body and hips wrapped in animal skins.

I froze while clutching a rock I was about to use on the second cage's locks. I was looking at a young fae—her arms were out and her fingers wiggled as enormous sheets of water erupted from the stream and crashed into the swelling mass of invisible daemons. Their cover was blown, making it easier for my team to fight them.

Screams erupted from the thinning crowd of Imen I'd just released. More daemons had come in and were slashing at them with their bare claws. The water fae with platinum hair swooshed in that direction, launching powerful jets of water at specific daemons to help the Imen escape. I exhaled sharply, glad to have another fighter on our side.

She was furious and feral, growling and clawing at the daemons between water hits. She bared her teeth and managed to get her hands on a couple of knives, using them to slash throats as she fought off the fiends chasing the freed Imen. I resumed my task and smashed open the two locks on the second cage, pulling it open.

They looked around, visibly confused since they couldn't see me, then ran after the others. They were all of different ages, both male and female. They wore animal skins similar to those on the water fae. Two of them even seemed to recognize her, their eyes widening before they rushed toward her—the others pulled them away to keep them from getting involved. That was a wise move, as the young fae was busy shooting water jets at daemons and cutting them with her knives.

What was a fae doing on this planet? Were there more of her kind, on other parts of the continent? I cursed under my breath as I found myself asking more questions, instead of finding answers for the ones I already had about this place.

Meanwhile, Hansa had just reached the third cage, one foot resting on a dead daemon's chest as she broke its locks and pulled its door open. Twenty more Imen came out, crying and screaming. They ran after the others.

I could see tears rolling down her cheeks as she fought off a few more daemons, then moved to the fourth cage. I wanted to help her and let her know I was okay, but I got sidetracked by a sturdy armored daemon that had just escaped Blaze's spiked tail. I stabbed him in the stomach, and he painfully realized I was there as some of his blood sprayed me. He charged me with his broken spear, his face contorted with fury and desperation.

This was his last attempt to kill one of us, and I was more than happy to make sure he failed.

25

CAIA

(DAUGHTER OF GRACE & LAWRENCE)

I never fully mastered controlling the other natural elements, as I'd always been strongest and most proficient with fire. But I managed to draw water from the stream in flimsy jets to help with revealing the daemons I saw coming toward me. I held my ground, oscillating between fire and sword attacks, using the stream whenever I caught a second in between.

I'd heard Hansa scream a couple of minutes earlier, but I didn't see what happened. I only caught glimpses of her furiously taking down more daemons, growling as she swung her broadsword around, drawing blood and severing horned heads.

Two daemons came at me just as I noticed the fae flying in over the brook and pushing water over the invisible hunters. I let loose on the fire side, sending out two blazing columns that swallowed the fiends whole. They screamed and wailed as their skin burned, until Avril jumped in and severed their heads, putting them out of their misery.

"What the hell is happening?" I shouted, dodging a spear from an incoming hostile.

"They... They got Jax!" Hansa cried out, shoving her sword through another daemon's throat.

Claws tightened around my heart as I looked around. I couldn't see Jax anywhere.

This can't be...

"Where is he?" I managed, launching another round of fireballs, while Avril and Heron finished the daemons off. I tried to find him, even on the ground, among the daemon corpses, but there was no sign of him.

Hansa stilled, frowning as she quickly scanned the area around her and came to the same conclusion.

"I... I don't know," she croaked, her eyes puffy and her lower lip trembling.

I heard a clang and saw Imen escaping from the fourth cage. My pulse raced as the conclusion of our fight got closer with every passing second. A buzzing sound caught my attention. I glanced up and saw the tracking spell at the end of the open area, where the gorge's walls tightened back toward the west. It glowed and hummed, then darted off to the right, toward a redwood cluster that masked several crevices.

"The tracking spell!" I yelled.

We were too busy surviving and fighting off daemons to follow it. But based on the speed with which it had suddenly decided to move, Fiona was very close.

What is going on here?

Everything was happening at once, and I had trouble processing. Jax was missing. The Imen were running free. We were all fighting a constant stream of daemons. There was a water fae helping us. The tracking spell had caught Fiona's trail. And all hell was about to break loose, as Blaze was less than a minute away from letting out the devastating fire from his throat.

I didn't even have time to experience anger or dismay. I barely had a second to shoot out more fireballs before stabbing another daemon in his side, right after he lunged and failed to hit Avril.

Then I paused, holding my breath. I noticed movement by the trees where the tracking spell had vanished. Fiona popped out of a crevice, drawing her long knives and running toward us.

"Fiona!" I screamed, my heart bursting with joy. Relief washed over me.

At this point, nothing could stop me. Two more daemons charged me, but I fashioned a thick fire whip and lashed it around, blocking rapier and spear hits with my swords as I advanced through the hostile crowd to get to Fiona.

She looked well, healthy and in one piece, with her hood and mask on—her eyes flaring with determination. She jumped in, slashing and hacking left and right with her blades. We met in the middle and took advantage of a few spare seconds to hug.

"Holy hell, Fiona!" I gasped, clutching her shoulder with one hand. "How'd you make it back here? Where have you been? Are you okay?"

"I'm good, don't worry!" She grinned, then nodded at Blaze. "I'll tell you everything once this is all over. Why isn't he burning everything down?"

"There were Imen in those cages." I pointed at the empty enclosures, then at the Imen running in the distance. Fiona followed my gaze, then frowned and took a deep breath.

"Okay." She nodded. "Let's get out of the way, then. There are way too many daemons still standing here!"

"Everybody out of the way!" I shouted to the rest of our team. "Fire in the hole!"

My heart thudded with the joy of seeing Fiona again and the excitement of watching all the daemons burned. We ran for cover, with Avril and Heron following us.

"Good to see you, Fi!" Avril breathed as we made for a cluster of tall rocks.

"Oh, you have no idea how good it is to be back!" Fiona replied.

We jumped over the boulders and hid behind them. I

could see Blaze from that angle, straightening his back and stretching his long neck as spears flew at him. They were, of course, useless, given his thick skin and sturdy scales.

I saw Scarlett and Patrik hiding inside one of the crevices, as did Harper and Caspian.

Hansa was still fighting a daemon. Blaze's throat swelled. He stretched his wings and cast a heavy, dark shadow over the gorge. If she didn't get out of the way, she'd be in the line of fire.

"Hansa!" I yelled.

She was pulled out of the way by something invisible, and dragged behind one of the limestone slabs closer to the eastern side of the gorge. My stomach dropped. I realized what had happened to Jax. He'd used the daemons' prime hunting tool against them. I knew he carried the invisibility spell ingredients with him, but it hadn't occurred to me that he'd been carrying them already mixed and ready to use.

The water fae caught my attention. She was still fighting daemons, hitting them with violent water jets and puncturing their jugulars with a sharp knife. She'd been pushed to the side, about fifteen yards from our position.

Blaze roared, and his jaws cracked open, a bright orange light erupting from his throat.

Oh, crap!

The fae was going to be obliterated there. I ran out. I had to save her. She didn't stand a chance.

"Caia, no!" I heard Avril scream after me.

I moved as fast as I could and flicked my lighter open. The fae was left with one daemon, while the thirty or so others tried to go after our team, scattering across the now-open field.

I threw my fire whip out and lashed it at the daemon, knocking him back several feet. His face burned red from my hit. He growled and moved to come after me as I grabbed the fae's hand. She gasped, and I followed her gaze. Blaze released his destructive flames in a titanic column, aimed twenty feet from where we were.

"Hold on!" I shouted, and fashioned a large fire sphere from my lighter, pulling her close to me.

She obeyed and wrapped her arms around my waist, holding me tight as the dragon inferno spread out like a devastating flood, burning everything in its path. Blaze roared again and let out another firestorm. I held my ground, my flaming sphere protecting us from the conflagration.

Everything burned in his path. The dragon bent forward on his front claws, his gathered wings twitching as he spat another blazing round. The daemons didn't even get to scream. The combustion was so sudden, so powerful, that they were instantly disintegrated.

The hellish rain went on for a few minutes, until every daemon had been reduced to ashes.

It all burned down. Every tree, every shrub, every creature that didn't think to run as fast as it could from the giant dragon, they were all gone, leaving behind black wisps and carbonized bones. I cleared my fire sphere as soon as I heard Blaze's grunt during his transformation.

"Are you okay?" I asked the water fae.

She gave me a wide-eyed nod, then both our heads turned toward Heron, whose painful groans were suddenly audible. He and Avril had left the stone refuge we'd found together—and I quickly understood why. The fire had been so powerful on that side that it had toppled the limestone slabs, leaving Heron, Fiona, and Avril vulnerable.

Heron's leather suit was burned on its back side, leaving parts of his skin exposed and severely injured. He'd covered Avril with his body to protect her from the fire. She dragged herself out from underneath him, and breathed heavily as she tried to assess his wounds.

Fiona had made it into the crevice behind, but Avril and Heron hadn't. Everything must have happened too fast.

We ran toward them as the rest of our team emerged from their hiding places.

26

HANSA

I was dazed. I'd been pulled out of a fight with a daemon. I'd seen a curtain of fire come down as I was dragged behind a large slab of limestone. I was lying on my side, a heavy body protecting me from the heat. Sweat bloomed on my forehead nonetheless, as Blaze's inferno had bumped the temperature up by several degrees.

My heart weighed a ton, my stomach burning as I remembered the past ten minutes. Where was Jax? Had he died with those daemons? Had he been killed earlier?

I didn't even think to see who had gotten me out of the fire's way.

"Did you really believe I'd be foolish enough to leave you behind and get myself killed?" Jax's voice trickled in my ear.

I stilled, realizing whose arms were holding me tight,

whose body heat was enveloping me. My pulse started racing, my chest about to burst. I turned around and saw Jax reappearing as his invisibility spell wore off.

Of course... He used the invisibility spell. He took a page out of the daemons' playbook.

His jade eyes scanned me from head to toe as he helped me stand.

"Are you okay?" he asked, his mouth and nose still obscured by the mask.

I nodded slowly, readjusting myself to reality. Anger soon replaced the temporary relief I'd felt upon seeing him alive. I now wanted to kill him for putting me through hell, for letting me think he'd been torn to shreds by daemons. My fists balled at my sides, but I said nothing. I saved my wrath for later because I was even more thrilled by Fiona's return.

I'd seen her just before Jax had dragged me away. I hadn't even had a chance to relish the sight of her, seemingly unharmed.

I left Jax and ran straight for the girls, who gathered around Heron. Patrik handed Blaze a pair of pants from his backpack. The water fae stood silently a couple of feet away, while Scarlett, Avril, Fiona, Caia, and Harper were kneeling around Heron. Caspian was next to Patrik and Blaze. The gorge around us was coated in dark ashes, the limestone walls covered in black.

Avril was looking after Heron, who'd suffered serious

burns during Blaze's firestorm. Mara and vampire blood would cure him fast enough, though, so I scratched that concern off my list. Fiona stood up, beaming at me.

I rushed toward her and took her in my arms, holding her tight. I let out a long, tortured sigh.

"You have no idea how good it is to see you," I whispered.

"I could say the same thing," she replied gently. "I'm sorry I went ahead in that tunnel... What happened to you back there? I didn't even hear you after it collapsed."

"I got knocked out... I don't know by whom, but that tunnel was deliberately blown apart." I frowned, pushing her back and resting my hands on her shoulders. "What happened to *you*? Caia and Blaze had you in that prison, then lost you to a daemon... We came here looking for you."

"I know." She nodded. "I'm sorry, Hansa... I... It happened so fast. I'll tell you all about it in a bit, I promise. We need to get as far away from here as possible. More daemons will come, eventually."

I hugged her again, relief washing over me and soothing my ragged nerves. My team was back together, and, with the exception of a few serious flesh wounds, they were all okay. We'd made it this far into the gorge without getting killed.

My whole body hurt, and tension was still gathering in the back of my head, as I glanced at Jax. I'd thought him gone. I'd thought I'd seen his body being ripped apart and flung around, chunks of raw, bloody flesh hitting the hard, dusty ground. I'd thought I'd lost him to daemons, and the pain had been unbearable. It had fueled a rage I hadn't experienced since the war with Azazel. Since I'd cut off Goren's head in exchange for what he'd done to my tribe, my sisters... my daughters.

The agony was familiar. The grief had eaten away at me over the course of about fifteen minutes. I wanted to punish him for making me feel like this. I needed to hurt him the way he'd hurt me, or worse. I needed him to feel as ravaged as I'd felt when I'd seen him vanish into a vicious crowd of daemons.

I loved him. And I wanted him to feel the brunt of it, too.

You don't hurt me and expect to walk away unscathed.

27

AVRIL

(DAUGHTER OF LUCAS & MARION)

I slit my palm and pushed it against Heron's lips, to help him heal from the deep third-degree burns on his back and legs. We'd already assessed back on Calliope that Mara and vampire blood had similar properties, especially where healing was concerned. The intensity of Blaze's fire had caught us by surprise. We'd thought we'd be safe behind those rocks, but the sheer blast and the temperature were so intense, we had to dash into the crevice just twenty feet in front of us.

Fiona had managed to slip into it, with just the tips of her hair and parts of her suit burned. I went in second, but my move had coincided with Blaze's second wave of fire. Heron had pushed me to the ground, shielding me with his body. He'd sustained serious wounds, his leather suit burned and portions of the skin on his back simply gone.

He drank from my palm, his eyes closed. He breathed heavily between painful groans. My insides burned and my stomach had been reduced to the size of a pebble, watching him in such agony. I knew he'd be okay, but still, it was torture to witness his suffering. I could only imagine what those wounds felt like.

Fiona and Scarlett were on their knees next to me. They both took fistfuls of healing pellets out of their belt compartments and crushed them over Heron's burns. The fine pink-and-yellow powder scattered gently over the raw flesh, then dissolved and bubbled up as it was absorbed into the tissue.

Hansa, Harper, Caia, Blaze, and Patrik were a couple of feet away, giving us room to breathe. The young water fae who had helped us stood next to them, watching us quietly. I couldn't see Caspian anywhere anymore. Which was strange, given the fact that he'd only just been with us. Harper looked confused as well, but didn't say anything. I tried to focus on what our team had to do next, including questioning the water fae, but my mind refused to cooperate, unable to function properly until Heron was healed.

"You're going to be okay," I murmured in his ear, my right hand resting on the back of his neck while he continued to suckle from my palm.

Jax moved closer, a frown pulling his brows together.

He'd sustained some injuries as well, in the form of long gashes on his sides and thighs, but nothing that wouldn't eventually heal on its own in the next couple of hours. He fumbled through his belt pockets and found more healing pellets. He swallowed one and gave the rest to Scarlett and Fiona, for them to keep applying over Heron's wounds.

"Hang in there, little brother," he said slowly. "We need you."

Heron groaned, his eyes shut tight as he tried to stay conscious and concentrate. His lips were soft against my skin, his fangs gently grazing my palm as he drank my blood. I ran my fingers through his short black hair, slowly massaging his scalp in a bid to help him relax.

"Thank you for looking after him, Avril," Jax said.

"It's okay," I replied. "He saved me just now. It's the least I can do…"

"You could do more," Heron huffed, resting his head on the ground for a while as the healing pellets and my blood settled in his system and began repairing every inch of damaged tissue.

My cheeks caught fire at the sound of his low and husky voice. I knew he had a dirty joke ready to follow up with, and it was the one time I was okay with letting him be his naughty, unapologetic self.

"Oh, yeah? And what's that?" I asked, feigning irritation.

His jade eyes peeled open. He looked at me and flashed me a lazy but charming grin.

"I can't talk about it in public," he muttered. "It's frowned upon in civilized societies."

"Since when did that ever stop you?" I chuckled, then continued massaging the back of his neck. Patrik handed me a red pill made of dried herbs and crystal salt, then nodded at Heron.

"It's for pain relief," the Druid said.

I gave it to Heron, letting it slip between his lips.

"Here, swallow this for the pain," I told him.

He sighed and chewed the pellet a couple of times before swallowing it with a bitter grimace.

"It tastes like crap," he complained.

"Yeah, well, maybe don't get your ass scorched next time!" I retorted.

"I'll do it again if it means keeping you safe," Heron mumbled. His gaze found my face, and our eyes met. I softened at his words, and the thought of his selfless gesture cast him in a different light. Sure, I already knew what a valiant and noble creature he was beneath his philandering persona, but watching him nearly die to save me was something else entirely.

My heart swelled in my chest, and I swallowed back tears, slowly coming to terms with the fact that I'd nearly lost Heron in this gorge. It wasn't an easy thought to process. On the contrary, it felt like torture, like claws puncturing my gut and slashing my chest open.

"Thank you," I whispered, not sure whether he heard

me. I just needed to say those words, to acknowledge his sacrifice.

"Anytime, baby," Heron breathed, closing his eyes and smiling again.

I had a feeling the pain medication was kicking in, and it had an interesting effect on him. His neck muscles relaxed under my grip, and he emptied his lungs with a long sigh.

I was shaken to my core, downright rattled by the turn of events. I'd been so busy fighting alongside Heron that it had come as a given that I would see him walk out of this mess unscathed. Watching him lie on the ground, his back and legs slowly healing from what had been horrific burns up until five minutes ago... That had not come up as a possibility.

Blaze came closer, his arms crossed over his chest. He looked terrible. His blue eyes were filled with regret, and his lips pressed together in a thin line.

"I am so sorry," he said with a trembling voice. "I thought you were all covered. I didn't see you, so I thought you... I thought you'd made it to safety..."

"Oh, Blaze, it's okay!" I tried to comfort him. I hadn't thought to blame him at all. There was no reason for that. "We picked the wrong place to hide, that's all. We should've gone directly for that crevice, but everything happened so fast."

"I should've been more attentive." Blaze shook his head, not yet ready to accept that he wasn't at fault for this.

"Listen, Blaze," Heron groaned, then slowly rolled to his side to get a better look at the dragon. "This job comes with risks. It really wasn't your fault; we had to finish those daemons off once and for all. It's why we brought you with us in the first place. Now, stop beating yourself up over this, and just get comfortable with the fact that I'll kick your ass six ways from Sunday once we're back in the training halls."

Blaze gave him a weak smile.

"Cool," he replied, "but don't expect me to make it easy for you. Bring your best game and I'll be happy to let you beat me."

I stifled a chuckle as I noticed Heron gradually regaining his strength. We'd made it this far, after all. There was no way I was letting him die in these gorges.

There's no way I'm letting you die, period.

28

HARPER

(DAUGHTER OF HAZEL & TEJUS)

Sometime in the brief interval between Blaze's dragon inferno and our emergence from our safe spots, Caspian had vanished. One minute he was standing next to me as we came out of the crevice, my legs still trembling from both the sight of the dragon's full power and the proximity of Caspian's body. The nook we'd slipped into was narrow, and its tight walls had kept me glued to him, his heart thundering against my ribcage.

I'd been so busy struggling to regain my footing and normal breathing that I didn't even notice when he left. He'd clearly done it on purpose; otherwise he would've at least had the decency to say goodbye or something. I'd used my True Sight to find him, while we gathered close to Heron and Avril, but I couldn't spot him anywhere.

I couldn't understand why he'd done it, either. We were going to meet later, back in Azure Heights, anyway. Had he thought that his "job" of assisting us was over? Was he planning to wait for us back in the city, to see if we emerged with a full and perfectly functional team? I couldn't put it past him, based on his previous statements.

While Heron healed, lying in Avril's arms, we all looked at the young fae. Judging by the abilities she'd briefly displayed during the fight, I had a feeling she was a water fae. Her platinum hair was long and braided over her shoulder, with blue feathers and beads, and she wore brown leather sandals reminiscent of ancient Greek styles, with straps tightened up to her knees, matching the rest of her outfit. Her skin was tanned, and her eyes were a bright blue that spoke of tropical oceans.

She repeatedly glanced over her shoulder, frowning as she watched the freed Imen become black dots in the distance. The prisoners we'd released had already reached the western plains.

"Thank you for helping us," Hansa said with a soft smile. "My name is Hansa. What's yours?"

The fae eyed us carefully, her arms crossed over her chest.

"Vesta," she replied.

"What brought you here, Vesta?" Hansa asked.

"My family was in these cages." She shrugged, nervously stealing glances at Heron and Jax. "I was coming to try to get them out when you started fighting the daemons. Thought I'd help."

"That's strange, I didn't see any fae in the cages," I replied. "I'm Harper, by the way, and these are my friends and family. So, if there's anyone who understands the courage it took for you to do what you did, it's us. Seriously, thank you. You helped us move things along."

Vesta nodded slowly, then asked, "What's a fae? My family are not fae. They're Imen, of the Free People."

"How is that possible?" I asked, confused. Fae were either born or made, but there was no sign of fae cultures on Neraka, nor had I read anything about their presence here in the Exiled Maras' library.

"I don't know," she sighed. "I only remember the last five years of my life. I was found by the Free People, floating toward the ocean shore. I was unconscious and wounded. They nursed me back to health. They gave me shelter and helped me start a new life in their tribe. Coming here to save them was my duty."

"But you know what you are, right?" I replied.

"You said 'fae'. What's that?"

"Fae are special creatures, deeply connected to the natural elements. Water, earth, fire, and air," I explained. "They're a highly capable species, treasured across this universe. But fae are usually born fae, and only in very rare instances are they made. Which is why I found it odd when you mentioned your Imen family."

A moment passed as she digested the little bit of information I gave her. She seemed enlightened, her eyes glimmering with curiosity. She finally had a name for herself, for her abilities and her different nature, and an explanation for her uniqueness among the people who had found and helped her.

But her presence there still begged the question of her origins.

"You're a fae, too?" Vesta asked Caia. She seemed particularly fascinated by my cousin, and, after what Caia had done to protect her from Blaze's firestorm, it made sense. Of course, fire couldn't kill a fae, as it was an element they controlled, but the intensity of a dragon's flames could still cause serious damage.

"I am only part fae, and I'm more on the fire side." Caia smiled. "I'm guessing you're more into water?"

Vesta beamed with pride, her lips stretching into a grin.

"So, you live in the west, beyond these gorges?" Hansa asked.

"Yes. The Free People are safer in the woods there, but the daemons still hunt us," Vesta replied, a muscle twitching in her jaw as she looked around at the charred daemon corpses. She then settled her gaze on Blaze, awe twinkling in her eyes. "You're a dragon..."

"You've heard of dragons?" I asked, wondering how much the Imen knew of the world beyond Neraka.

"From old wives' tales, yes." Vesta nodded, then sized Blaze up for a second. "But none of them looked this good!"

We all burst into laughter, while Blaze's face reddened up to his ears and he gave us a sheepish smile. Heron's cackle was particularly loud.

"Don't even think about it, little fae," Heron replied. "The dragon's keeping himself chaste for another couple of years."

"Shut up and focus on healing." Avril chuckled as she reprimanded him, helping him sit up as his burns transformed to first-degree blotches of red skin. "You loudmouthed bully!"

Vesta appeared amused by our friendly banter, but continued looking over her shoulder and giving Jax and Heron the wariest of looks.

"What's wrong, Vesta?" I asked her.

"Nothing, I... I just need to get back to my people," she replied slowly. "They're out there on their own, and I need to make sure we all reach the woods before more daemons come out. Everything you've done here will have an impact on us, though you were only trying to help. Not blaming you or anything, but my tribe needs me now more than ever."

She bowed before us and moved to go after her people, but Hansa wasn't ready to let her go yet. None of us were. She knew more about the daemons than anyone else we'd come across—except, of course, Caspian, who kept his cards close to his chest.

"Wait, Vesta," Hansa said, "what about these daemons? Where did they come from? Where were they going? What do you know about them and their underground cities?"

Vesta opened her mouth to respond, but the sound of horses trotting echoed through the gorge and caused her to fall silent. Her blue eyes widened when they found the source of the noise. We followed her gaze and noticed Exiled Maras pouring out of a narrow pass, fifty yards away, on the other side. Vincent and Cadmus led the group with their swords drawn. They crossed the open space, staring at the burnt tree stumps, the charred daemon corpses, and the columns of black smoke still billowing around us.

I then heard feet shuffling, and, as soon as I turned my head, I saw Vesta running as fast as she could toward the western part of the gorge, after her people.

"Damn it!" I cursed under my breath, using my True Sight to follow her. She glanced over her shoulder at us, fear visible on her face whenever she looked at the Correction Officers.

"Do we go after her?" Scarlett asked, ready to dart in the fae's direction.

"No." Jax shook his head. "She's scared of Maras. It's why she was looking at Heron and me with such fear. We need to go back to Azure Heights now, send one of us to Calliope to bring back more troops before we try to engage the Free People or take any action against the daemons."

"For now, however, we need to make sure we all reach the city in one piece," Hansa agreed.

We watched as Vincent, Cadmus, and the Correction Officers rode their horses across the burnt ground.

"Let's not tell them about Lord Kifo." I remembered Caspian's request for discretion. "I... We promised we'd keep our mouths shut."

Hansa nodded but was sure to make her groan heard. She wasn't too happy with the secrecy, and I couldn't blame her.

"What about Lord Kifo?" Fiona asked.

"He's the masked dude who's been sort of helping us out," I replied, oversimplifying for lack of time. "I'll tell you more when we're alone."

"Oh. Wow. Okay," Fiona breathed, blinking several times as she connected the dots.

"We'll have to talk about him as soon as we get a chance, though," Hansa said. "This secrecy makes us no better than the Exiled Maras."

"I agree, and we will definitely discuss this later," I replied, then moved closer to Fiona and wrapped my arms around her. "You know, it's been so crazy and chaotic here that we haven't even had the chance to hug you and tell you how good it is to see you, Fiona."

She giggled as Scarlett, Avril, and Caia joined in for a group hug.

"Thank you... Thank you all for coming to get me." Fiona gave us a warm smile.

"What happened to you out here? How'd you make it back?" I asked.

Vincent reached us first, and got off his indigo horse with a radiant smile plastered on his handsome face.

"It's a long story. Hold on." Fiona sighed, then looked at Lord Roho, who rushed toward her and took her in his arms, holding her tight against his chest.

"I can't believe they found you!" Vincent breathed, his face hidden in Fiona's auburn hair. He caressed her face, affectionately looking at her before he placed his hands on her shoulders and looked her over from head to toe. "Are you okay? Are you hurt?"

"I'm good, thank you, Vincent." Fiona gave him a weak smile.

The Exiled Mara looked thrilled to see her again. But I couldn't help but wonder how much he knew about what was really going on in these gorges, as well as beneath them.

The doubts I'd had about the Maras before were only coming back twice as strong now, virtually blaring in the back of my head after what Caspian had told us about the daemons. He obviously knew more, so why wouldn't I think that the others knew more too?

29

FIONA

(DAUGHTER OF BENEDICT & YELENA)

"Vincent, Cadmus, what the hell took you so long?" Jax growled, eyeing Vincent and the Correction Officer I identified as Cadmus. The other Maras stayed behind, unable to take their eyes off the devastation left behind by Blaze. The smell of burnt flesh was impossible to ignore.

"It wasn't easy to find another access route to this gorge." Cadmus shrugged, then jumped off his horse. He glanced at me. "Are you all okay? It looks like you've made quite the mess here..."

"We heard the dragon roaring from the other side," Vincent added, then glanced around. "What *happened* here?"

"Daemons happened," Harper replied, nodding toward

Blaze as he moved closer to Caia's side. "But we had a dragon, so, you know... Poof!"

"Fiona, where were you?" Hansa shifted her focus back to me, as the question of how I had made it back to them had yet to be answered.

"A daemon took me from the prison, as you already know," I explained. "His name is Zane. He kept me in a cage, inside a grotto nearby, in another gorge toward the north side of this place. It was weird, though. He used colored powders, which he blew in my face, to either knock me out or render me unable to move—"

"Wait, colored powders?" Patrik interjected, his eyes narrowing as if he were trying to remember something. "What colors were they?"

"Well, he had three," I recalled, scratching the back of my neck. "A yellow one that knocked me out altogether. A red one that relaxed my muscles too much, to the point where I could barely use my arms and legs. And an orange one that paralyzed me. It kept me conscious, but I couldn't move or even speak."

"That's swamp witch magic." Patrik frowned, then glared at Vincent and Cadmus. "And this wasn't the first time I've seen daemons use it, either. Their invisibility is also a swamp witch spell. We think they used charmed collars to control pit wolves. How did daemons get their claws on this kind of magic?"

"What are pit wolves?" Vincent asked. His expression

was blank, as if he'd barely registered what Patrik had just said.

"Wait, hold on." Hansa raised her hands to slow the conversation down. "Let Fiona finish first, and we'll get to the swamp witch magic in a second. One issue at a time. Let's focus."

They all looked at me, waiting for me to tell the rest of my abduction story.

"Okay, so, long story short, Zane kept me there for a while. He even fed me; he gave me blood. He said he wasn't sure what he was going to do with me, but, in the end, he decided to bring me back here because you were all spotted by other hunters," I replied. "He said he'd seen the dragon back at the prison and the only reason he took me in the first place was because, and I quote, I 'smell delicious' to daemons and he didn't want to 'share' me with anyone. According to him, I would've been taken one way or another. In hindsight, it's actually better that *he* took me, since I'm back here now."

"So, what, he brought you back here because he didn't want to get on our bad side?" Blaze asked, slightly confused.

"Kind of, yeah." I shrugged. "Honestly, he wasn't all that open or willing to talk, so I can't exactly explain his reasoning. He left me inside a crevice nearby, and I knew how to get to you from there."

"I guess I should thank him for bringing you back to me." Vincent smiled, unable to take his eyes off me. The

Mara seemed over the moon to see me again. It was heart-warming, to a certain degree.

He'd been nothing but good to me, and he sure knew how to use his charm around me. He still made my heart flutter a little bit, but, given all the questions still lingering around him and the rest of his city, I couldn't help but put on the brakes and keep a safe emotional distance from the guy.

"Speaking of Fiona and our journey here, what happened with the tracking spell?" Harper asked, pulling her hair up in a ponytail with one of the elastic bands she kept on her wrist. "It stopped for a while, hovering, before it darted over to Fiona."

"I'm not exactly sure," Patrik replied. "I've never used the spell before Neraka but my guess is that Fiona was still in one location, while the light orb was tracking her and it stopped and hovered for a while as Fiona was probably moving."

"When the daemon brought me back," I murmured. "The spell is more accurate when the person it's tracking is standing still, then."

"That kind of makes sense," Harper replied, satisfied with our conclusion.

"And what happened here?" Cadmus asked.

Heron stood, his arm around Avril's shoulder.

"We were looking for Fiona and came across a daemon convoy," Hansa said. "We fought invisible ones earlier, but this group was organized. They had armor and weapons. They were pulling four cages with captured Imen. They had giant black beasts, called pit wolves, with red eyes and swamp witch collars. They're even faster than the daemons and just as vicious. We managed to set the Imen free, and, once they were out of this area, we let Blaze loose. As you can see, there are no survivors."

"Stating the obvious there," Cadmus muttered.

"The daemons are much better organized than we originally thought," Jax replied. "And they're using swamp magic. How is that possible? I thought the swamp witch only gave you a handful of mild charms along with that interplanetary travel spell."

Vincent and Cadmus looked at each other, but their expressions were quite different. Vincent was confused, his eyebrows arched and his green eyes wide. Cadmus, on the other hand, was silent and didn't show any reaction to what we'd just told him. He either knew about the swamp witch magic or he'd been trained to wear that straight face twenty-four seven, just like Caspian. Based on what we'd seen so far, however, it was difficult to tell.

"Cadmus," Harper said, her voice low, "if you know anything about this, now's the time to tell us. We're getting tired of finding things out on our own here, and trust me, if you keep holding out on us, GASP won't be so kind going forward."

Cadmus glanced at her, his gaze softening for a second before he resumed the harshness he'd previously displayed.

"The daemons are *organized*. They don't just hunt," Hansa reiterated. "They go out in armored groups, with giant beasts and cages, and capture dozens of Imen at once, to take them to their *underground cities*. Please, tell us what you know."

"This is something that you'll have to take up with the Five Lords," Cadmus replied, getting back on his horse. "I'm not privy to such information, nor was I aware of what the daemons were doing. I doubt the Lords will know more, but it's the only suggestion I can make at this point."

"Are you implying that the Five Lords *know* about all this?" Jax asked, gesturing around him.

"That's not what I said." Cadmus scoffed. "I merely suggested that you take these issues up with them, not with me. I'm but a foot soldier and a servant of the city."

A minute went by in absolute silence. The Maras were still looking around, while occasionally stealing a glance at Blaze, as if putting a face to the devastation left behind. The sun was going down at this point, and the gorge was cast in dark shadows, while threads of black smoke still reached for the purplish sky.

"Ready to go?" Vincent moved closer to me, his arm snaking around my waist.

I nodded. He smiled, then took the reins of his indigo horse and brought the animal near.

"Vincent, wait," Harper said, frowning. "There's something you should know."

He waited, one hand resting on the stallion's strong neck. Harper sighed and pulled a couple of folded papers from her back pocket.

"We came across Sienna on our way here," Harper said.

I blinked several times, as did Vincent. This was news to both of us. A flurry of questions flew through my head, but I kept my focus on Harper and took Vincent's hand in mine. I had a feeling he might need emotional support of some kind, given that Sienna wasn't with us now.

"What? Where is she? Is she okay? Isn't she coming home? Did daemons take her?" Vincent pretty much voiced all my questions in one breath, his brow furrowed.

"Vincent, she wasn't kidnapped." Harper let out a sigh, her shoulders dropping. "She ran away. She met one of the daemons prowling on the first level a few months back but told no one about him. According to her, they fell in love and knew that your family would never accept them, and—"

"Wait... Hold on..." Vincent shook his head, unable to process the news. "What do you mean, she met a daemon? Do you mean to tell me she *knew* what was happening here? She knew that daemons were taking our people and said nothing? You're lying. That cannot be. My sister would *never* do such a thing!"

Vincent quickly shifted from befuddlement to anger.

Not that I could blame him, given what Harper was telling us about Sienna. To think that she knew, and told no one, was simply horrible.

"She couldn't tell anyone," Harper replied. "Tobiah, the daemon she fell in love with, would have been killed by his own people if Sienna revealed their existence. She ran away with him, and they're temporarily living in the Valley of Screams, hiding from both daemons and Maras. Nobody knows they're together. Tobiah pretends she's his game, to keep other fiends at bay. And she's not coming back to Azure Heights, either. She gave me this for you. I'm sorry, Vincent..."

She gave him the papers, which Vincent unfolded and scanned briefly. His lips parted as he recognized his sister's handwriting. His fingers trembled while he read her words, clutching the thin sheets and trying to make sense of what Sienna was telling him.

I leaned in to get a good look, but couldn't read the entire message before he folded the papers again and shoved them into his coat pocket. He straightened his back and regained his composure, putting on a calm face. He gave Harper a nod.

"Thank you," he muttered. "I will pass this on to my mother."

We all looked at him for a while without saying anything. What could be said, anyway? His sister had vanished, causing nothing but grief to his family. She'd chosen love over everything else, hiding out here in the Valley of Screams in order to protect herself and the daemon she'd fallen for.

But she had blood on her hands. All the Maras and Imen abducted during the time she'd spent meeting with Tobiah in secret—their deaths were all on her. She could have said something. She could have at least left a note for her brother and mother, before she ran away.

I looked at Vincent and recognized the grief in his eyes. I couldn't voice my thoughts about her now. He needed time to process it all, to come to terms with his sister's choices. And we had enough on our plate already.

He tightened his grip on my hand, then gave me a soft glance and guided me to the saddle.

"Let's go," he said, his voice hoarse. "The sun is coming down, and we need to get out of here before midnight, when the beasts usually come out. I reckon the first daemons we encountered had caught our scent, for them to have come out during the day. The ones you dealt with afterwards were an exception, given their transport, because they seem to prefer hunting at night... I believe the Druid has to try that protection spell for the city again?"

"Yes, among other things." Patrik nodded.

Harper let out a sharp whistle that echoed throughout the open space of the gorge. Horses neighed not far from us, and, soon enough, six indigo mounts emerged from the eastern part of the ravine, where the path narrowed again.

I got on Vincent's horse first, and he climbed behind me. His body felt warm against my back, his thighs gently pushing mine as he took the reins with one hand and rested the other on my hip. It felt nice and safe, and, after the madness I'd experienced over the past sixteen hours or so, I was grateful to be able to lean back and find him there to support me.

30

SCARLETT

(DAUGHTER OF JERAMIAH & PIPPA)

P atrik and I shared an indigo stallion again as we all
headed back to Azure Heights. It was somewhere
close to five in the evening, and the sky was darkening
above, while shadows stretched from every tree, stone, and
shrub scattered through the gorge. The wind rustled
through the leaves, carrying echoes of screams from several
miles away.

More daemons were coming out, tormenting their
victims and further consolidating the name of this wretched
area. The Valley of Screams held many secrets, but we'd
been able to uncover a handful since last night. We knew
more now than we had when we left the infirmary.

I was getting a little too comfortable in the saddle, with
my back virtually dissolving into Patrik. After the night and

day we'd had, however, I decided to not overthink this, and just enjoy the feeling of being so close to him. It soothed me in ways I'd never thought possible. My muscles were relaxed, and my head was incredibly clear, putting the pieces of our entire Nerakian puzzle together in new combinations that made more sense.

His breath tickled my ear, while I gazed ahead, my focus sharp on the several miles left until we reached the eastern plain.

"I want to thank you for everything you did today," Patrik murmured.

His voice rumbled through me, setting off vibrations in my stomach and tingles along my spine.

"It's okay," I replied, my voice barely audible. "It's my job, after all..."

"That's true, but you're incredibly good at it, and I imagine I owe you my life, Scarlett."

Several seconds passed while I tried to think of a decent response. Funnily enough, the clarity I'd experienced earlier was gone, replaced by the fuzziness that his deep voice generated inside me.

"You showed exceptional critical thinking, as well," he added, and brought an arm around my waist. He pulled me closer to him, and only then did I realize that I'd been slowly sliding forward a few inches. "The way you handled the pit wolves was, by far, a noteworthy highlight of your performance."

I'm practically melting... Sheesh...

"You sound a little too stuffy for what we've just been through," I murmured. "Why don't you just go ahead and say that I royally kicked ass back there? It sounds more... realistic."

I had to defuse some of the tension building inside me because of his hold on me. I could almost hear the smile in his voice.

"Okay then, Scarlett, you royally kicked ass today," he replied gently, making me giggle.

I exhaled in an attempt to relax, but all I managed to do was further sink into his body. His heart was thumping against my back. I glanced around, looking for something to talk about—anything that would keep my mind off my position. I needed to resist what I was feeling because Patrik was still in mourning and in no shape or mood to even consider a rookie like me for another relationship.

I caught a glimpse of movement somewhere to my right. I turned my head and saw two bright red eyes. My muscles instantly tensed, my senses flaring. I gripped the handle of my sword. I then saw the full form of what I'd noticed and stilled, holding my breath.

It was the pit wolf I'd accidentally freed earlier, huddled behind a large slab of limestone. It looked wary and curious, its nostrils flaring when its gaze found mine. I straightened my back, but Patrik didn't let go. Instead, his forearm dug into my stomach as he reaffirmed his hold on me.

"I think it's best if we leave that creature be," Patrik whispered in my ear.

I immediately looked up at him, and noticed him watching the pit wolf. He'd seen the beast, too.

"Why? It tried to kill us, do you think it's wise?" I replied slowly, then glanced at the creature again. I hadn't had a chance to test my theory regarding the collars on another pit wolf earlier, so I was a bit wary about its presence there. My brow furrowed as I tried to understand what it was doing here. It was perfectly quiet and hidden, just watching us as we moved past it through the gorge.

"I've already taken the broken collar with me," Patrik breathed, careful not to make himself heard by anyone other than me. "I'll study it back in the city, but, from what I can tell at first glance, it acted as a behavior modifier. I mean, look at the pit wolf now... It looks genuinely harmless and scared. It knows not to charge us; it's already seen what the dragon can do, and we clearly outnumber it. Its body language speaks of fear."

I nodded, then looked at the road ahead once more, leaving the pit wolf behind. Patrik had a point, and, if my musings about the collar proved to be true, then I certainly didn't want the blood of an innocent animal on my hands.

A couple of minutes slipped by, and I felt myself relax again.

"You know, you were pretty darn awesome back there, too," I said. "I mean... The way you jumped between spells while blocking attacks... The speed with which you cast your magic was truly a sight to behold... I've never seen such prowess, not with so many hostiles at once, while dodging attacks from giant pit wolves and avoiding getting stomped by a dragon. I have to say, it takes seriously mad skills to do what you did."

I held my breath, realizing I'd just droned on about how cool he was. I glanced up and found his gaze settled on my face, warmth exuding from his steely blue eyes. His lips stretched slowly into a self-assured smirk that was both cute and incredibly sensual—though I was pretty sure he wasn't aiming for the latter.

"Scarlett, are you giving me a compliment?" he said, playfulness twinkling beneath his long black eyelashes.

"I... I guess so, yeah," I croaked. "Why, is that a problem? Do you function better with negative feedback? Because I can tell you the exact opposite, too. I can express dismay at your two left feet, your inability to coordinate between fire and water spells, or whatever else I can come up with, and... I should stop talking now."

I pressed my lips together, once again amazed at how my mouth functioned ahead of my brain. He chuckled, his gaze softening as he studied every feature of my face—from my eyes all the way down to my lips. A little ball of liquid heat got itself stuck in my throat, and I was unable to look away.

"I appreciate both positive and negative critiques." His smile filled me with sunshine, and it was a feeling I never wanted to let go of. "So please, by all means, if there's ever something you feel I might be faltering with, do tell me. Your opinion matters to me."

"Why... Why does it matter?"

"Because you are, by far, one of the brightest creatures I've ever come across. It isn't just your physical speed that stands out, but also the velocity of your mind, the way you process and interpret everything you learn. It's always a pleasure to watch."

His forehead smoothed as he shut his mouth. The look on his face suddenly changed, from bright and amused to blank and just too serious for the lighthearted tone of our conversation. He sighed, then peered somewhere in the distance, breaking eye contact and allowing an invisible wall to fall back between us.

It hit me then what had just happened. Patrik had just told me he'd been watching me.

He'd mentioned observing my physical speed *and* mental processes. All this time I'd thought I'd been invisible to him, and yet he was actually studying me. Analyzing me. Drawing conclusions about my intelligence and athleticism.

He's been watching me. He's been listening to me. He's been forming opinions... thoughts about me...

The idea was completely unexpected. I'd convinced myself that Patrik wasn't looking my way at all, not even for a basic assessment. And I had a feeling he'd just said more than he'd intended, judging by how quickly he went silent and looked away.

"Thank you," I murmured, then leaned back into him.

There were only a few miles left between us and the eastern plain, and I wanted to spend them in the warm safety of his arms. I wanted to go over everything he'd just said, and figure out what was happening in his head.

I then remembered the dream he'd mentioned after Minah's death. A dream that involved me. We'd yet to talk about it. This wasn't the right time, but I needed to find a good moment to get him alone and ask him about the dream and my presence in it.

Why was he dreaming about me? Why was he watching me? Why was he paying attention to me?

I'd hoped I'd come out of the Valley of Screams with fewer questions about everything. Leave it to Neraka to double down and give me more to think about on my way out.

31

HARPER

(DAUGHTER OF HAZEL & TEJUS)

I was at the front of our reunited group, riding on Caspian's horse. To my surprise, he'd left it behind. Jax and Hansa were next to me, sharing an indigo mount, while Scarlett and Patrik were right behind us, along with Caia and Blaze, Avril and Heron on separate horses, and Vincent with Fiona. Cadmus and the Correction Officers stayed at the back, their eyes constantly darting around the gorge as they looked for any signs of movement. There was still the risk of invisible daemons coming out before we made it back to the field.

Screams echoed from behind, their frequency increasing with each hour that passed, as if the Valley of Screams were angry and lashing out for what we'd done to its horned inhabitants. More creatures were falling victim to the daemons, but there was nothing we could do at this time. Even with a dragon, we needed more literal firepower to launch a full-scale attack.

The daemons were much better organized than we'd initially assumed. We were now dealing with two classes of hostiles—the invisible hunters and the armored fiends. It got worse if their ranks included pit wolves, creatures that scared and fascinated me at the same time. I couldn't help but wonder whether there were other beasts in their ranks. Worse, even more vicious creatures that obeyed the daemons.

I shuddered, and I felt Caspian's horse react beneath me. It was a beautiful stallion, with peculiar blue eyes and a long white mane combed to one side. It was strong, and, judging by the length of its legs and its strong muscles, it was perfectly capable of impressive speeds. I stroked its neck, and it gave me a huff in return. It liked my touch.

I couldn't get Caspian out of my head. He'd followed us deep into that gorge, he'd nearly gotten himself killed to help us, and then he'd vanished without so much as a good-bye, and even left his horse behind. Surely I'd see him again in Azure Heights, but still, his behavior baffled me. He switched from cold to hot, then back to freezing when I least expected it.

There was a slight pang in my stomach whenever my mind wandered toward him. He rattled my senses and stirred emotions I'd never thought I'd experience—a confusing ensemble of anger and excitement, all at once. Was I starting to like him? Was *that* the reason I was having such a hard time keeping my cool in circumstances that required a clear head?

He was a dangerous creature to fall for. He'd helped us so far, but he kept way too many secrets. I didn't like being kept in the dark, not when so many lives depended on me and my team. Regardless of his motives, Caspian didn't seem to trust me, and I sure as hell wasn't willing to trust him in these circumstances—at least not beyond what we already knew about each other.

One thing was clear, though: I wasn't the only one he was keeping secrets from. The other Lords, and even his Correction Officers, seemed to be in the dark, as well.

I glanced over my shoulder and got a quick look at the rest of our team, Vincent, Cadmus, and the other Maras. We were all quiet, the air between us and the Exiled Maras thick with tension and distrust. The more we uncovered about this place, the sketchier they looked, even when they swore they had nothing to do with daemons. But that swamp witch magic came from somewhere, and, according to their own records and accounts of the past, the only swamp witch to set foot on Neraka was part of the Druid delegation.

The air rippled behind us. I heard feet shuffling on the ground.

"Daemons!" I shouted, my instincts immediately kicking

in as my heart jumped into my throat. We were in for another rough tumble.

I caught glimpses of red eyes emerging from crevices on both sides, as well as from behind. The Correction Officers drew their swords, and Caia whipped out her lighters, while we closed our ranks and drew our nervous horses together.

"Blaze, let some of that fire out," Hansa said. "Keep them away, and let's speed up. The plain is less than a mile away!"

Blaze jumped off the indigo horse and slapped its rump, prompting the animal to neigh and run ahead, darting past us at great speed, with Caia still on its back.

"Blaze, be careful!" Caia yelled, concern furrowing her brows.

We all nudged our horses and galloped through the gorge, racing for the opening just eight hundred yards away. I looked back and saw Blaze bursting into full dragon form. The daemons were left behind and forced to face him as he filled the entire space between the gorge's limestone walls.

He growled and exhaled a column of fire that spread out and engulfed the daemons in amber flames. I heard screams and wails. The daemons hadn't stood a chance. Blaze roared and released a bright orange inferno, the flames licking at the walls as they consumed everything in their path.

We galloped through the last hundred yards of the gorge, and I breathed a sigh of relief once my horse reached the tall grass of the eastern plain, the mountain rising tall and proud in the distance. Its lights twinkled, its white marble buildings glimmering in the early evening shade. The sky was a deep purple, with a faint orange glow beyond the Valley of Screams, where the sun had set.

We made it...

More roars erupted from the gorge behind us, but we kept going. Caia was right in front of me, constantly looking over her shoulder, and frowning as she saw the dragon fire fill the ravine and scorch trees, bushes, and the dozens of daemons we'd left behind.

I thought the fiends had learned their lesson by this point. We had a dragon, and we'd killed plenty of daemons in two short-lived battles already. Yet they persisted. Were they stupid, or were they simply relentless and hopeful?

Halfway through the plain, I heard Blaze's giant wings flapping before I saw him flying overhead, his enormous shadow covering us for a split second. I checked the back again and saw thick black smoke billowing as burning daemons spilled out from the gorge. Some had made it into the stream, but I doubted they had enough strength left to come after us.

We reached the main road leading up into the city just as Blaze landed on the infirmary level and shifted back to his original form. We met him outside on the outdoor platform, just as one of the six Correction Officers still guarding the perimeter gave him a cloak to cover himself.

I got off my horse and went straight to one of the Maras standing next to Blaze.

"Has there been any suspicious movement while we were out?" I asked, and the Correction Officer shook his head.

"Did your people seal the tunnels?" Jax came up next to me, briefly scanning the terrace.

"It's currently in progress," the guard replied.

"I'll go check and report back within the hour," Cadmus said, still on his horse.

"Please do that." Jax nodded. "The sooner you have the underground tunnels sealed, the better. Patrik will prepare the protection spell again, for us to apply to the underground level as well, just to be sure."

"I shall see you shortly, then," Cadmus replied, and motioned for his group of Correction Officers to follow.

They trotted up the street, then spread out and scattered throughout the city's upper levels. Fiona slid off Vincent's horse and joined us in front of the infirmary door, while Patrik disabled the protection spell he'd cast upon it.

"Will you be okay?" Vincent asked Fiona with a concerned expression.

She gave him a weak smile, then nodded and placed a hand on my shoulder.

"I'm always okay, one way or another," she replied softly.

"Good," he sighed. "Now, if you'll excuse me, I have to break the news regarding Sienna to my mother. I hope to see you all later, and, should you need my help with anything, please don't hesitate to ask."

He then rode his indigo horse up the main alley toward the top. We left the six Correction Officers behind and went inside the infirmary, where the dead daemon and Minah were still well preserved under Patrik's Druid magic.

"Okay, there is clearly a lot we need to go over," Jax said as we gathered around the table, which still had maps of Azure Heights and the Valley of Screams spread out on top of it.

I remembered the meranium medallion that Caspian had left for her, and fished it out from my back pocket, then put it around her neck. "Wear this at all times, it'll stop daemons from eating your soul. Won't stop them from trying to kill you, though," I murmured.

"Thanks." she nodded, offering a faint smile in return.

"Let's start with Fiona. What details can you tell us about the daemon who took you?" Jax asked.

"He was way stronger than me, which kind of says something," Fiona replied, placing her hands on the table and leaning onto them. She looked tired, and frankly, I couldn't blame her. She'd been through quite enough in the span of twenty-four hours. "He wasn't very chatty, but he was extremely confident in his abilities and those of his people. He repeatedly said we're in over our heads here."

"He and Caspian would get along great, then," I muttered. "Great minds think alike, after all."

"I don't know anything else about him, other than his name," Fiona continued, staring at the map of the gorges, her gaze tracing our route along the stream, which was marked with a thick blue ink line. "He had tattoos on his upper body, and I imagine they represent some kind of social status among the daemons."

"Which would make him superior to our friend over here?" Heron asked, pointing at the dead daemon. Only then did we notice the ten black markings on his upper arm, obscured by smudges of dried blood. They were tattooed into his tanned skin in a vertical sequence of squares, triangles, and circles.

"He definitely had more tattoos, covering his arms and chest. It would be reasonable to assume that, yes." Fiona nodded slowly, her eyes narrowing as she analyzed the daemon's marks. "Zane had a cave in the gorge next to the one I found you in. He was fiercely protective of it, and didn't even allow other daemons to get close. He went out after them as soon as he heard movement outside. There's a hot-water pond in there, and he keeps a fire burning for warmth. And I spent most of my time in a cage."

"Would you be able to find it on the map?" Jax asked, following her gaze as she looked for it.

"I can try... or at least give you an approximate area," she replied. "To reiterate, first he knocked me out with the yellow powder, as soon as we got out to the plain last night. I woke up in the cage and, naturally, tried to pry the iron bars apart so I could get out. He'd yet to reveal himself to me at the time. He blew red dust in my face, and my limbs just turned to jelly. I could still move them, but I lacked my usual strength. That's when he showed himself to me, by bathing in the pond."

"Yeah, we found out that trick after we tested the elements on this bad boy," Patrik said, his arms crossed over his chest as he stared at the daemon.

"Glad to see you had a specimen to work with." Fiona gave him an appreciative smile. "Otherwise you would've gone in blind, and that really would have sucked for us all... I can't believe it's swamp witch magic, though. I could've sworn it was some feature of the daemons as a species..."

"It's not identical to the invisibility spell we use." Patrik frowned. "And I didn't get any samples, not from this daemon, nor the others back in the gorge. It all unraveled too fast before Blaze burned them all down."

"Maybe they altered it or something, because I know for a fact that the invisibility spell shouldn't be sensitive to water." Hansa pursed her lips.

"That might be a possibility, but I think we need Viola and the swamp witches' magic tome to verify it." Patrik shook his head slowly.

"And you said the dusts he used on me were also swamp witch-related?" Fiona asked.

"Yes, definitely. They're part of a series of stunners, as the swamp witches called them. Ten powders in different colors, made from certain crystals and prepared with specific incantations. Each serves to disable parts of or the entire body, and has a direct impact on a creature's nervous system," Patrik explained.

"That makes sense," Fiona muttered, then shifted her focus back to the map. "But they don't last for too long, and Zane didn't seem to take that into account. I felt the effect of the red dust wear off and managed to escape as soon as he went out to confront some daemons."

"I thought you said he let you go," I said, slightly confused.

"Yeah, he did." She nodded, then gave me a half-smile. "I was out of the cave and running when daemons caught up with me. I got injured in the process, and they actually over-powered me. One of them started eating my soul..."

I gasped, my eyes wide. I stared at her, and pain clawed at my heart at the thought of her suffering.

"Damn..." Heron breathed. "How are you still standing?"

"Zane got to me." Fiona shrugged with a pained expres-sion, as she recalled the string of events leading up to her release. "He killed the daemons and brought me back to the cave. I blacked out, I was in so much pain. I can't possibly describe what it feels like to have something gnawing at your soul. I didn't even think it was possible for a vampire to suffer like this. Thing is, I only had chunks of my soul consumed. Zane gave me his blood to drink, and it sped the recovery process. He said that, in the absence of daemon blood, it would take a long time for me to heal."

A couple of seconds went by as we all processed the information, while Fiona stared at the map.

"What is it about daemon blood that heals your soul?" Hansa asked.

"It probably has to do with the fact that he consumed souls, as well. The soul itself is pure energy. Once absorbed into the bloodstream, it functions as fuel for the organism. So, I basically ingested bits of someone else's soul through Zane's blood, and healed mine," Fiona replied. "After that, he blew orange dust in my face to shut me up and keep me still, and brought me to that part of the gorge where I found you all. He said he didn't want us to spend too much time in there, basically, because our dragon was making a big mess. He sounded as if he couldn't be bothered to deal with us. He didn't seem scared at all..."

"Did he say anything else?" Jax scratched his growing stubble and pinched the bridge of his nose. He, too, was tired.

"Not that I can remember," Fiona said. "But if something else comes to mind, I'll be sure to tell you. I'm still reeling from it all, to be honest."

"Can't blame you," Avril replied, putting an arm around her shoulders. "We'll get you to bed early tonight; you need to take it easy. At least for a few hours."

"What about Vesta?" I asked, looking at Hansa and Jax. "What was up with that?"

"I know, I'm equally baffled." Hansa raised her eyebrows. "I didn't expect to come across a fae in these lands..."

"Can we even guess how she made it here? She looked very young," Caia added.

"And she *really* didn't like Maras," Heron muttered. "I mean, with me and Jax it was slightly different because she'd seen us fight, but as soon as she heard and saw the Correction Officers coming in, she darted."

"I have no clue whatsoever," Hansa replied, resting her hands on her hips. "But we could try to look for her in the coming days. I was hoping we'd come up with some answers from this expedition, but it seems like all we got were even more questions."

"The most pressing one being: how the heck did the daemons get their claws on such complex swamp witch magic?" I sat on the corner of Patrik's bed, my shoulders dropping. I wasn't tired, as my entire body still buzzed with Caspian's energy, but I was feeling mentally exhausted. Everything got murkier with every step we took, and it didn't look like it was going to clear up anytime soon. "And Caspian split as soon as the fight was over... I can try to press him for some answers. After all, we *did* survive the gorge."

"Yeah, what happened to him? How did he vanish like

that? He even left his horse behind, didn't he?" Heron frowned.

"I don't know." I shrugged. "Maybe he just didn't want to be around when Vincent and his Correction Officers found us. He did stress the importance of our discretion regarding his involvement."

"That does make sense," Hansa mused, then clapped her hands once. "Okay, everybody go back to the inn. Have a hot bath, freshen up, fix your suits, replenish your combat resources, grab some blood and some food on your way out, and let's meet back here in a couple of hours to discuss an action plan. In the meantime, I imagine Cadmus will be back and will confirm whether all the underground tunnels were sealed."

We all nodded and moved to leave the infirmary. I walked out last, glancing over my shoulder to see Jax and Hansa left inside. I closed the door behind me, then walked across the terrace to Caspian's horse. I'd left the indigo mount grazing one of the flower pots, and it was still there, bright red petals occasionally popping out as it chewed them over.

I brushed its strong neck with my fingers, and it nudged my head with its nose in response. I couldn't help but giggle as it sniffed my hair, then huffed with delight.

"Time to take you back to your master, don't you think?" I asked the creature, gazing into its left eye, mesmerized by its deep blue.

I climbed onto its back as it neighed and clicked its front hooves against the brown cobblestone. I gave it a gentle nudge with my heels, and it rushed onto the alley leading up to the Lords' mansions.

My heart was starting to do its own sprint inside my chest. I felt slightly nervous at the thought of seeing Caspian again. I had so many questions for him; I needed to put them in a reasonable order so I wouldn't overwhelm him.

Hopefully, he'll answer this time. He promised he would if we survived the gorge, and, well, here I am. Still standing...

32

HANSA

As soon as the door closed after Harper, I stilled. The anger I'd experienced earlier, in the gorge, after Jax revealed himself as still very much alive, came back in waves of hot red. My blood simmered, and my heart twisted itself into a painful knot.

Jax moved slowly toward me, his jade eyes wide and hazy.

The tension between us was so thick that I could cut it with my broadsword. Except that, with the rage coursing through me, it wasn't the tension I was willing to slash into. I'd spent a good quarter of an hour thinking Jax was dead, while fighting daemons and struggling to free the Imen prisoners. Those had been the longest fifteen minutes of my life. I was raw on the inside.

"Hansa, I'm sorry I gave you a scare in the gorge, but—"

I slapped him so hard my palm hurt. He grunted as his head shot to the side, and he nearly lost his footing. I'd lost a whole tribe and my own daughters just three months earlier. I'd fallen for Jax, and he was giving me this hot-and-cold routine that was already driving me up the wall, only to leave me in temporary hell, thinking I'd lost him too. There was so much pain, so much grief already piling up inside me. There was no room for anger in my heart. I had to let it out so I could breathe again.

My fingers, my whole arms trembled. I breathed heavily and glared at him.

He straightened his back and groaned as he touched the left side of his jaw. His skin was already turning red there. He pushed his tongue into his cheek, then made a grimace and clicked his teeth. He gave me a sad smile, then took another step forward.

I was so mad at him. But I was also glad he was still standing. I felt tears coming to my eyes, but there was no way in hell I was going to let Jaxxon Dorchadas see me cry. I inhaled deeply and tried to get my anger under control.

"Hit me again, Hansa," he said, and I sensed the tremor in his low voice.

I frowned, trying to deal with the bundle of emotions cluttering my throat and making it difficult for me to breathe in his presence.

"Hit me as many times as you want," he added, calm, his arms stretched out from his sides. "I deserve it, I know…"

"I thought you were dead," I hissed, still livid and trembling from every single joint.

"I know." He nodded slowly, his gaze fixed on my face. "It all happened so fast. I had to do something drastic, and I didn't have time to tell you. It would've been counterproductive, anyway... I am sorry, Hansa. It seems like no matter what I do, I still end up hurting you."

Tears burned my eyes, and I felt my whole being caving in, chunks of me collapsing with painful echoes. I swallowed it all back as my heart took over. My brain blacked out. I closed the distance between us, and I pressed my lips against his.

His breath hitched, while I held mine. I'd thought he was dead. I'd thought I'd lost him, and we hadn't even kissed. We hadn't even touched one another in an intimate manner. I'd yet to feel his lips on my skin, his soul entwined with mine. This was the least I could do to soothe my own pain, my own fears of losing him.

I needed to feel him.

Just to get an idea of what his lips might feel like.

Bliss...

Before I knew it, Jax's arms tightened around my waist, pulling me closer as he deepened the kiss. A thousand suns exploded. I closed my eyes and lost myself. His heart thundered against me, and I couldn't help but moan as his mouth consumed mine.

The intensity was more than I could handle, but I didn't want it to stop, either.

This had been three months in the making, and we could both feel it. There was fire coursing through my veins. My flesh tingled as one of his hands moved up, tracing my spine, until he gripped the back of my neck and groaned, his tongue working mine in endless circles.

He exhaled sharply and pulled himself away, blinking rapidly as he struggled to catch his breath. The jade pools of his eyes were dark and soft, his lips tender and plump. He took a couple of steps back, running a hand through his hair, and cursed under his breath.

"This *really* isn't a good idea, Hansa," he managed, his voice low and raspy.

I took several deep breaths, still relishing his scent. It filled my lungs and made my senses expand like newborn stars. It took me a while to regain full consciousness.

"What... What exactly isn't a good idea?" I croaked.

"This... Between us," he replied, guilt pulling his brows closer together. "I've already proven that I'm highly capable of hurting you without even intending to do so. I don't deserve you, Hansa, and you don't need more pain in your life. You really don't."

I paused, wondering whether I should slap him again or focus on the tears that were quietly making their way back up. I bit my lower lip, to the point where it hurt and I nearly drew blood, trying to find the right words to tell him every-

thing I was feeling. We'd never really put names to our feelings. We'd been tiptoeing around each other since the war
with Azazel had ended.

I've had enough.

I was done putting up with his excuses. I was done with
his cowardice. We both felt it. It was there, hanging between
us like a big, red bubble that we needed to pop. I had feelings for him, and he had feelings for me. It was there in the
way he looked at me. I could feel it on his lips, in his arms
wrapped around me.

I was done pretending that it wasn't real.

"Screw this," I muttered, then threw my arms around his
neck and kissed him again. This time I leaned into him and
unleashed my succubus nature. I felt his chest pressing
against mine. He growled as he parted his lips and let
himself go, no longer able to control himself. I'd often struggled to keep my nature under control around him, but this
time I just couldn't.

I needed him to feel me—*all* of me.

He tasted like spiced rosewater and honey, sending me
over the edge as he gently bit my lower lip, then took over
my mouth once more. He breathed through his nose, his
eyes shut. His hands roamed freely up and down my back.
His fingers then gripped my hips, digging into my flesh and
pulling me closer, our tongues clashing as we devoured
each other.

Jax wasn't just responding to my kiss. He was reacting to

my succubus nature, and I could feel him shuddering in my arms. He wanted more, and he couldn't stop himself. I had that effect on him, and I was seconds away from pushing him into a physical frenzy.

But I stopped. I shut myself down, then pushed myself away.

My lower lip throbbed. My throat and my chest burned. My core was blazing, sending heatwaves through my limbs. But I had to put an end to it. I just needed him riled up to the point where he could acknowledge how powerful this thing between us was. My succubus nature didn't work like it did for the rest of my species—though I'd never told anyone about it. I could only amplify what was already there.

My sisters could get anyone to fall head over heels for them, to lose control in their presence. I could only influence those who already found themselves attracted to me. Given my looks, however, it was hard to find someone who didn't find me beautiful, who didn't desire me. But I knew, deep down, that the reactions that Jax displayed under my influence were all his, simply boosted to a much higher intensity.

He let out a tortured sigh, his shoulders dropping as he leaned against the table behind him. He was highly aroused and befuddled, his eyes twinkling as he stared at me in disbelief. I had never let myself loose on him like this before, and not for so long. Our little episode at the ball could barely qualify as a "taster", a mere sample. He'd never experienced my full succubus effect.

"Let *that* sink in for a while," I said, gritting my teeth and trying hard not to unravel before him, "before you tell me this is a bad idea. Come talk to me when you're ready to act like the leader you *are*, not the coward you've been acting like."

I opened the door, welcoming the evening breeze as it caressed my face and soothed my spiking temperature. It pained me to see Jax like this, but I couldn't let him break my heart. This was going to end up one of two ways. Either we'd just had our first and last kiss, and things between us would forever be broken and sour, or we'd merely started a good conversation about what we wanted from each other, despite everything we'd yet to say out loud. One thing was obvious: this Mara needed some tough love to get the sense knocked back into his thick head.

"Someone needs to stay here and watch over Minah and the daemon until Patrik gets back," I said coolly. "So don't go anywhere."

I stepped outside, and the six Correction Officers stationed on the terrace gave me a brief nod as soon as they saw me.

"So, what? I'm grounded?" Jax replied from inside.

My eyes found his, and I had to work extra hard to keep my pulse from racing at the sight of him. He was so soft, so raw and intense, like nothing that he usually displayed. I wanted to pat myself on the back for having managed to bring out this tender side of him.

"You're damn right you're grounded," I hissed, then slammed the door behind me.

I stormed past the Correction Officers, then went up to the Broken Bow Inn. I passed my fingers over my lips—they were so sensitive, tingling with the memory of his kiss.

I need a hot bath. Or a cold shower.

33

HARPER

(DAUGHTER OF HAZEL & TEJUS)

I reached the stables behind the Lords' mansions and guided the horse to its enclosure, where servants had already left fresh water and hay. I stroked its neck and dropped a kiss on its nose. It huffed and nuzzled my face, and I found myself genuinely head over heels for the creature.

"I like you, too," I murmured, then looked around.

There was no sign of Caspian in his mansion, according to my True Sight. I frowned, wondering where he could be at this hour. I didn't want to think that something might have happened to him in the gorge, but a thump in my stomach forced me to consider it.

I checked every room, but only saw servants and a couple of Exiled Maras—young ones, most likely in their early teens. They were reading in a study, seated at a table surrounded by walls covered in books. I scanned the other mansions as well, hoping I'd catch a glimpse of him somewhere, maybe even visiting with Amalia Obara, the perfect blonde with sky-blue eyes and a perfect, ladylike demeanor.

Still, no sign of him anywhere.

"Looking for me?" Caspian's voice startled me.

I yelped, jumped a couple of steps forward, then turned around to find Caspian standing next to his horse's enclosure. His jade eyes glimmered with amusement as he took off his hood and mask. Only then did I notice the cuts in his black uniform, with traces of dried blood.

He'd already healed, but he'd definitely sustained his share of injuries during our battle in the gorge. I quickly regained my cool composure and put on a straight face. I didn't like displaying any kind of emotion, especially in front of Caspian. He had a way of using it against me.

"Where'd you slither out from?" I asked, raising an eyebrow.

He smirked, then moved closer. My body stopped listening to my brain, the muscles tightening as I tried hard to breathe evenly. Caspian was making it very difficult for me to focus.

"I have my secret access routes into the city," he replied. "I believe I've already shown you one."

"Oh, right." I nodded briefly. "Well, good to see you're back in one piece."

"Were you worried?"

That twinkle in his eyes persisted, while he kept a straight face. He was toying with me.

Two can play that game.

"No, I just feared you'd get yourself killed before you answered my questions." I shrugged, feigning boredom. "I don't like it when my investigative leads kick the bucket. It means I have to start all over."

The corner of his mouth twitched for just a split second, enough to make me wonder whether it was real or I'd just imagined it. I crossed my arms over my chest, uncomfortable with barely a few inches between us. His energy was still flowing through me, and it seemed to resonate with his proximity, to the point where I could almost feel my body hum gently.

"Speaking of which, why'd you run off without saying anything?" I asked.

"I didn't think you were one to care for manners," Caspian replied. "Were you upset I didn't say goodbye?"

"No, I just thought some invisible daemon might have survived Blaze's inferno and managed to snatch you and shove you in one of those crevices."

"The fighting was done," he said, his eyes fixed on mine. "You won. There was no need for me to be there anymore. Besides, Vincent and the others weren't too far away. I saw them on my way back through a neighboring gorge. I wouldn't have wanted them to find me there, anyway."

"Ah, yes, the secrecy!" I quipped, then offered a smug grin, befitting his overly confident attitude. "By the way, I'm not sure you noticed, but we all survived the gorge. So, pay up."

"Pay up?" He raised an eyebrow and mirrored my stance, bringing his arms over his broad chest. I felt tiny in comparison, despite my height and athletic physique. I also felt warm, a sensation I'd only experienced whenever I was near him.

"You said you'd answer my questions if I made it out of the gorge in one piece," I reminded him, slightly irritated. He made me foolishly nervous. "I'm here, so... spill."

Caspian took another step, bringing himself so close that I had to tilt my head back to be able to look in his eyes.

Big mistake.

I inhaled his scent and felt a little lightheaded. Slim ribbons of gold shimmered out of him, along with dark green and red tendrils—it was how his emotions manifested, to my sentry eyes. Now that I'd had a taste of his blood and I could see everything clearly, I was positive that I'd somehow cracked through his shell and tapped into his feelings. I'd been quite sure before, but now, hours later, there was literally no denying it. And I wasn't going to tell him, either. This was my little tactical advantage.

His gaze darkened as he looked at me.

"You only get one question answered," he said, and my lips parted in response. He noticed, but his eyes quickly found mine again. "You have until tomorrow night to formulate it, Miss Hellswan. Think it through and use it wisely."

"You're joking," I gasped.

"Do I look like I'm joking?" he replied, moving his hands behind his back.

"No, but seriously, are you joking?" I shot back. "After all I've been through? Not to mention I came back from the Valley of Screams with more questions than answers! I kept my word, and you said you'd answer my *questions*. Emphasis on the plural!"

He scoffed, looking away for a couple of seconds before shifting his attention back to me. My fists were balled at my sides, while my pulse had decided to go on a rampant sprint.

"You must understand that I cannot trust you so easily," he said.

"Really? Not even now? Have I not given you enough reasons to trust me, while all you've done is keep me in the dark?"

"Miss Hellswan, many lives depend on my secrecy," he replied bluntly. "Until I can assess your overall trustworthiness, you only get one question answered. You can take it or you can leave it. That is all I can offer right now."

A minute went by in absolute silence, as my blood simmered and I narrowed my eyes at him. I was tempted to argue over this, give him a piece of my mind, but, based on everything we'd seen and discovered in the gorges, I was better off with Caspian on my side—even if all I got were tiny morsels of information.

I thought this over, while my gaze traveled along the sharp lines of his face and settled on his lips for a brief moment. They parted slowly, prompting me to look up and find myself reflected in the jade mirrors of his eyes, his long black eyelashes casting their delicate shadows above. Ancient Greek sculptors would've considered him a masterpiece.

The dark green emotion I'd noticed earlier was now flaring at me, warning me. I understood then what I was seeing. It was distrust. He really didn't trust me. There was a mixture of fear and concern swirling around in him, flakes of red and yellow mixing with his wariness. At least he was being honest about his feelings, though I couldn't yet put my finger on that golden glow emanating from his pale skin —that was something else entirely.

One question was better than none, I figured. I let a heavy sigh tumble out of my chest and nodded, relaxing my hands and placing them on my hips.

"Fine, Lord Kifo," I muttered begrudgingly. "I'll ask one question. For *now*. But why are you giving me until tomorrow to formulate it? I can pick any of the dozen burning ones I've got lined up for you."

He cocked his head to one side, then gave me a half-smile that made me thaw like an ice cube dropped in hot water.

What is wrong with me? Get it together, Harper Hellswan!

"I'm simply giving you time, so you make sure to ask me the right question," he said softly.

I blinked a few times, trying to figure him out. It turned out that being able to read his emotions wasn't as cut and dry as I'd thought it would be. He still baffled me.

"I swear, I have a *really* hard time trying to understand you," I murmured. "It's incredibly frustrating, and I don't mean just you. You are extremely frustrating all on your own, before I even begin to analyze everything else around you. There's no better way of saying this, but you baffle me, Lord Kifo, and I fear I might get hurt or worse if I keep trying to figure you out."

It felt better to voice that thought. Some of the pressure in my chest went away. And Caspian seemed surprised by my sudden burst of honesty, but he quickly resumed his usual coolness.

"I am sorry, Miss Hellswan, that I am causing you such distress," he replied, his tone even. "But you can't possibly comprehend what I am being subjected to, on a daily basis, as a Lord of my House and City, and as an Exiled Mara looking to protect the innocent. I've been working in the shadows for a long time, and I cannot risk exposure to anyone. Not even you. Not until I am fully confident that you will not turn against me if I give you the whole truth. As it stands right now, you might not be able to handle it."

We gazed at each other for a while, keeping our words

and doubts to ourselves. I memorized every word of his statement, with the intention to go over it later that night. There was a lot he was telling me already, without any specifics. He was giving me a glimpse of his troubles without naming them.

Most importantly, I could see that his mistrust was authentic. I wasn't sure what else I could do to prove to him that he could trust me, but I decided to give up for the day. I had one question that I could ask, and I was determined to ask the right one.

"If you'll excuse me, Lord Kifo," I nodded briefly, "I need to head back to the inn."

He blinked once, slowly, as a way of acknowledgment, and watched quietly as I turned and left him there. I felt his eyes on me, the skin on the back of my neck prickling. The hum in my body gradually subsided as I reached the stairs leading down into the city.

I have but one question...

What did I want to know? What was the most important thing I needed him to tell me?

Yeah, not getting much sleep tonight...

34

CAIA

(DAUGHTER OF GRACE & LAWRENCE)

I spent well over half an hour soaking in the bathtub back at the Broken Bow Inn. I scrubbed the dirt and soot off with fragranced soap and hot water, allowing my muscles to relax and my skin to finally breathe. Even a fire fae needed to cool down after the inferno we unleashed in that gorge.

I had another suit left, leaving the other two to dry by the window of my bedroom. I slipped into it and geared up again—every day was intense, and I had to be ready for anything, twenty-four seven. I then went out, locking my room, and stopped in front of Blaze's door.

Might as well grab him on my way back to the infirmary.

I knocked, suddenly feeling a little nervous. I brushed it off and took a deep breath. I had to keep a professional demeanor in front of him. But then the door opened, revealing Blaze with nothing but a towel around his waist. Water droplets trickled down his tanned skin, and the dim lights cast sculptural shadows against his muscular torso.

My chest tightened as my eyes found his. My professional demeanor was hanging by a thread. His dark hair was still wet and curly, covering his forehead. We stared at each other for a while—though our motives probably varied a little. He appeared just as surprised to see me, and I couldn't look away because he was simply gorgeous.

I'm in so much trouble...

"Hey, Caia," he murmured. "What's up?"

"Um, well, I... I was just on my way down to the infirmary, figured you'd want to tag along," I said, then cleared my throat and produced a flat smile. I couldn't offer a full one—I wasn't great with multitasking in his presence, and I needed some focus to stop my heart from galloping like an indigo horse.

He didn't say anything. Instead, he held his soft gaze on me for about a minute, then nodded slowly. I pointed downstairs, over my shoulder, at the main entrance.

"I'll... Um, I'll wait for you outside," I replied, then walked over to the stairs.

I heard the door to his room close, and I felt like I could breathe again. Just being around him was suddenly so intense!

I found an empty seat on the small terrace outside and

laid back into it. Nocturnal flowers were blooming in nearby pots, while the first moon rose lazily over the city. Exiled Maras and Imen shuffled around, some on relaxed evening walks and others on their way home. The ocean breeze made the tree crowns shudder, their leaves rustling as the evening set in.

The whole day had been an amalgam of horrible and weird, on top of the previous night, which I'd already classified as "freaking crazy". We'd learned a couple things about the daemons, sure. We'd found Sienna, too, though her circumstances were nothing like we'd expected. We'd even gotten Fiona back, which was, by far, the highlight of the day. But there were still so many unknowns left.

Why was Caspian helping us? What was up with all the secrecy surrounding him? How had Vesta made it to Neraka? What else were the daemons hiding underground? What were the Exiled Maras doing with their prison—was it really just a detention center suddenly breached by the horned fiends, or was there something darker, more evil at work here?

The Imen's behavior was a little off, too. And the Lords weren't exactly sharing everything with us. We'd found that out the hard way when we discovered the prison, just as daemons strolled in for a midnight snack.

That jail bugged the hell out of me.

We should infiltrate it. We should find Demios, Arrah's

brother. If we remove the leverage over her, she may be willing to talk and tell us more about the inner workings of the city.

Because the Exiled Maras didn't know about Arrah's ability to withstand their mind-bending tricks, she was at risk. Technically speaking, they didn't need to imprison Demios to keep her quiet, since they probably thought they'd already mind-bent her into ignorance. Yes, speaking to Demios could definitely go at the top of our to-do list, along with sending one of us back to Calliope to get the rest of GASP involved.

I was so deep in thought, looking out into the distance at the dark plain and Valley of Screams, that I didn't even notice Blaze standing next to me. I jumped, startled by his sudden presence. He seemed amused.

"Sorry, didn't mean to scare you," he said.

"Nah, it's fine. My mind was somewhere else," I muttered, and got up.

We walked over to the main alley leading down to the infirmary. The silence between us was a tad uncomfortable —or at least, it was for me. I'd gotten a little too comfortable with his body so close to mine during our ride through the gorge, and my pulse seemed so quick to react whenever he came near me. The thought of talking to him about how I felt crossed my mind, but I feared this wasn't the right time.

"You were amazing back there." I decided to speak. There was no point in making things awkward just because

I had trouble understanding the depth of my feelings toward him. "Seriously, great job."

"Thanks." He gave me a shy half-smile, scratching the back of his head. I had a feeling Blaze wasn't great at taking compliments. It was cute. "Though I think I could've done better. I nearly burned Heron and Avril alive."

"Not your fault." I shook my head. "We knew we had to clear out, and we picked the wrong spot. It all ended well, so there's no need for you to feel bad in any way."

"Blaze!" Rewa's voice stopped us in our tracks. I couldn't help but sigh as we both turned around. Rewa nearly flew into his arms, hugging him tight and giggling with sheer delight. "I'm so glad to see you're okay!"

Blaze gave me what looked like an apologetic sideways glance, pressing his lips in a thin line as he gently pushed Rewa back, resting his hands on her shoulders. She was taller than me by at least a head, and yet Blaze still towered over her.

"It's good to see you too, Rewa," he said, his tone even and polite.

"You *must* join me for dinner tomorrow night!" Rewa beamed at him. "I've arranged for a wonderful feast for two, worthy of a champion of Azure Heights!"

Blaze blinked a few times, not sure what to say. I stepped over my own heart and gave him a friendly nudge and a discreet nod. Rewa had a thing for him, and we needed to keep him in her good graces if we wanted any inside information from the Five Lords. As much as I disliked the idea of Blaze going out with another girl, I had to support him and my team before anything else. My personal feelings were irrelevant.

"Okay, thank you," he replied with a faint smile.

"Great! I shall see you tomorrow at seven, then, at the Blue Butterfly." She fluttered her eyelashes at him, and I suddenly fought back a bout of queasiness. "It's on the eighth level. You can't miss it. It's only the most beautiful venue in this city."

"I'll see you tomorrow, Rewa." Blaze gave her a curt nod, then pointed at the top level. "Now please go home. It's nighttime, and we can't have you out on your own again. Not after what happened last night."

"Oh, you *do* care about me!" She giggled, clutching his forearm.

"Well, I care about not having your father's wrath rain down upon us if something were to happen to you." Blaze sighed.

"Okay, okay, I'll go home, then!" Rewa winked, then waved us both goodbye. "See you tomorrow, Blaze!"

We both watched quietly as she rushed up to the top level, her black dress shuffling over the cobblestones. I resumed my walk, unable to wipe the frown off my face. I thoroughly disliked this situation, biting my lower lip as I looked ahead, analyzing every shadow and every object on our path.

"I'm not happy about this either," Blaze said, his voice low.

I briefly glanced at him, then shrugged in my desperate attempt to seem cool with everything. I hadn't meant for him to notice my displeasure.

"I'm really not interested in her," he added.

"I know. It's cool," I croaked, not sounding as sure as I'd intended. "You're free to like whomever you want to like, anyway. You're a free agent. Just take care of yourself in the process. We obviously can't trust the Exiled Maras as much as we'd like."

He caught my arm, making me stop.

I looked up at him and felt my heart skip a beat. His dark blue gaze was so intense, I ended up holding my breath for several seconds. His grip on me was firm, yet soft at the same time.

"You should really stop thinking about Rewa and me," he said. "It's not going to happen. My heart will never be there."

He looked as though he wanted to say something else, as his lips parted. But his silence seemed to say something, too, and I melted like a candle in his hold. We stood like that for maybe a minute—a long and intriguing minute that I couldn't get enough of as our eyes stayed locked on each other.

I gave him a weak smile, then resumed our walk down to the infirmary.

It was getting harder to control my reactions when he was around. I didn't respond well to pressure, and being near him seemed to really test my ability to stay calm and composed. All I could think of was his handsome face, and the way his hair curled around his temples. I stole a glance at him as we reached the infirmary level.

Blaze was every girl's dream. Strong and noble, devastatingly handsome, and a friggin' dragon. No wonder they all swooned over him. But what about me? Was I swooning, too?

Nah, I'm... I'm pretty much melting.

35

AVRIL

(DAUGHTER OF LUCAS & MARION)

W e all gathered back at the infirmary at around eight. Our battle wounds had healed, and we'd settled the score with hunger, too, as the Broken Bow Inn provided blood and food for its guests. Patrik made it back first, giving Jax time to run to the inn and back, as well. The Druid had also prepared satchels to expand the city's protection spell to its underground level, and had laid out ingredients for the interplanetary spell on the map table.

Heron and Jax were the last to join us. I noticed the glances that Jax exchanged with Hansa. I had a feeling that the succubus had really laid into him earlier, judging by the puppy-dog look on his face. He looked as though he'd just been caught stealing a slice of pizza from the dinner table. My stifled grin subsided as soon as my eyes found Heron's.

He was particularly quiet, serious, and constantly staring at me. I realized then that I was looking at him differently. Sure, he was the same jokester and philanderer we all knew and... accepted, but he felt like so much more to me all of a sudden. My attraction toward him had been undeniable, but I'd pushed it back since Jovi and Anjani's wedding because I knew that getting together with Heron was a surefire way to have my heart broken.

And yet, there was a string tugging at my heart as I temporarily lost myself in his jade eyes. What I was feeling after all the events in the Valley of Screams was much deeper. I wasn't sure what to do with it. Heron hadn't changed. He had still been cracking his dirty jokes earlier, on our way back to the inn.

"Okay, now that we're all here," Hansa said, breaking my train of thought and prompting me to look away from Heron, "we need to split into teams again, to cover more ground. We still have a lot to do. First off, the city protection spell. Patrik has already set everything up; we just need to go down into the prison and bury the satchels in the north, south, east, and west walls. Fortunately, that can be done by a single team, as the bottom level is the one where Caia, Blaze, and Fiona were last night. I think Caia and Blaze can undertake this mission again."

Caia nodded, her hands behind her back, then gave Blaze a quick glance.

"I'd also like to request permission for us to try to find

Demios in that prison," Caia replied. "I strongly believe that Arrah's brother may help us convince her to help us. She knows more about the Exiled Maras than she's letting on."

"I can attest to that," I chimed in. "I think that once Arrah sees we're on her side, she'll come around."

Jax and Hansa looked at each other for a brief moment, then back at us.

"Well, then, let's do this the smart way," Jax said. "Fiona can use the invisibility spell, since we still have enough ingredients for at least five more short-term sessions, and look for Demios down there. You don't want to arouse suspicion from the Correction Officers. They'll all be busy keeping an eye on you during your protection spell preparation. Invisible Fiona can find Demios and sneak him out of there. Patrik can prepare enough of the spell for two."

"That makes sense," Fiona said, leaning against the window frame behind her, her gaze lingering on the daemon and Minah. "What about them?"

"We'll bury Minah in the morning," Hansa replied. "As for the daemon, I imagine Patrik wants to study him for a bit longer before we put him into the ground."

"Yes, I most certainly do," the Druid muttered. "He's got more secrets in there, for sure."

"Whatever we can find out about his species, we can use against them," Hansa agreed, then shifted her focus back to our group. "Right. Now, before we move ahead with our investigation and assessment of what the daemons have beneath the surface of Neraka, we need more GASP power. Which one of you vampire ladies is willing to ride the light bubble back to Calliope tonight? Harper, Scarlett, Avril? We can't let Blaze or Caia go. We need our Maras here with us. I can't leave the team, and neither can the Druid. So that leaves us with you three."

Scarlett, Harper, and I looked at each other for a while. I gave them a wink, then raised my hand.

"I'll go," I offered. I figured the several hours I'd spend in that light sphere, while moving across the universe, might help me put my thoughts about Heron in order. Maybe I could even talk about it with my mom while our troops gathered for Neraka. Surely she could offer some useful advice, or at least tell me to just get it out of my head because it only spelled trouble. I was already telling myself that, so maybe she could reinforce that thought.

"Fair enough," Hansa replied, and Patrik gathered the interplanetary spell ingredients from the table, while Jax opened the infirmary door for him. "Let's go."

She walked out, along with Patrik and Jax, and I followed. I passed by Heron, and he caught my arm, a dark shadow settling on his face. His gaze softened on me.

"Be careful, Avril," he murmured.

"I'm just going home and back. It's cool." I gave him a weak smile, unable to keep my heart from recklessly pounding beneath my ribs. He frowned, then inched closer to me.

"Have a safe journey. We've only done this interplanetary spell once; pardon me if I'm not comfortable with watching you go on your own," he replied, then let me go.

"No need to worry about me, Heron," I breathed. "I'm a big girl."

I went out, and the rest of the team joined us on the terrace. The Correction Officers stationed there moved back, giving Patrik the space he needed to prepare the spell. He drew the chalk symbol on the brown cobblestone, then placed the powders and herbs in their designated places.

"You're good to go." Patrik gave me a reassuring smile.

I nodded, then briefly hugged Scarlett, Harper, Fiona, Caia, and Hansa, and waved goodbye to the guys.

"We'll see you soon, Avril," Hansa said, one hand resting on her hip. "Just tell Derek and the rest of GASP everything we've learned so far, and they'll make the right assessment as to how many agents to send over. Just make sure they bring in more dragons, too."

I chuckled as I moved inside the chalk circle, facing my team.

"You *really* like the dragons, huh?" I winked.

"Who doesn't like giant lizards that spit out fire and destruction?" Hansa shrugged, then offered a playful grin. Blaze was blushing, even his ears turning red.

"I'm right here," he croaked, and we all burst into laughter.

"Yeah, I can see you," Hansa replied, patting him on the back. "Just take the compliment!"

I took a few deep breaths as they all looked at me again. Patrik muttered the swamp witches' interplanetary spell, and shortly after he finished, I was swallowed by white light in the form of a sphere. It hummed and buzzed for a minute before it allowed me to see outside.

They were squinting, the sphere shining brightly in front of the infirmary. It lifted me off the ground, making me wobble before I fell backward and was reduced to an accidental sitting position. I watched as my team got smaller, the interplanetary spell gaining altitude.

The city's lights glimmered gently against the dark backdrop of the mountain, with streetlamps scattered on every level and lining each alley and set of stairs. I looked up, watching the dark blue sky expand overhead, myriads of stars waiting to greet me in space.

The purple asteroid belt twinkled in the distance, stretching from the east to the west in a lazy arch. It kept its distance from Neraka's atmosphere. The light sphere trembled as it picked up speed, swishing toward the vast cosmos above.

Time to kick back and enjoy the view...

36

HARPER

(DAUGHTER OF HAZEL & TEJUS)

We all saw the light sphere take off and go up into the night.

It went smoothly for about thirty seconds. It shrank as the distance between it and Neraka's surface increased.

Then it exploded into a bright yellow flash that rippled across the sky.

It was followed by a loud bang and our gasps and screams, as we helplessly watched the disaster unfold.

My stomach dropped, and I clutched my throat, heat burning through me as if I'd been up there with her.

"Avril!" Heron roared, frozen in place.

Blaze darted toward the edge of the terrace. He leaped over the stone fence and burst into full dragon mode, stretching his wings. His clothes were torn to shreds, blown away by the wind.

"Avril…" Fiona breathed, tears glazing her eyes.

We were all stunned and broken. I could barely breathe.

"Stay here," Jax urged Heron, holding him back, though the Mara desperately tried to free himself and go after her. "Blaze will handle it. There's nothing you can do."

"She… Avril… I… I have to…" Heron was at a loss for words, pale and stricken with horror and grief. Tears rolled down his cheeks, his lower lip trembling as he tried to keep it together but failed miserably.

"Blaze will get her." Jax tried to reassure him, but the tremor in his voice left room for doubt.

We couldn't do anything other than wait. Fiona dropped to her knees, sobbing. Scarlett and Caia got down and held her close, no longer able to control themselves, either, as tears sprang to their eyes. The pain was almost palpable, and it burned through my chest, clawing at my heart.

I used my True Sight to follow Blaze as he cut through the sky at high speed. I followed the smoke trails left behind by the explosion, and saw Avril falling.

"She's up there—she's falling," I breathed, my fists balled and tightening till my nails pierced the skin on my palms and I drew blood. I yelped when Blaze managed to catch her on his back, breaking her fall, then turned around and glided back toward the city. "He got her! He got her!"

The girls jumped back to their feet, their eyes wide and suddenly hopeful.

Blaze landed on the terrace with a bone-chilling growl, and lowered his head. Heron pushed Jax off and rushed to get Avril off the dragon's back. He scooped her into his arms and brought her over to us, while Blaze shifted back to his original form. The Correction Officers were fearful of his presence, but one still found the courage to remove his cloak and give it to Blaze for cover.

Avril was severely burned, her skin red where it wasn't completely missing. She was unconscious, but I could still hear her heartbeat. It was strong and willing to put up a fight.

It'll take a lot more to kill you, Avril...

Her leather suit was destroyed, just patches clinging to her body here and there. Heron put her down and bit into his palm, lifting her head slowly. We gathered around her.

"Come on, beautiful, drink," he murmured in her ear. "I'm here, Avril, I'm here... Just drink and you'll be okay... Drink."

Avril's eyes peeled open. She moaned from the pain, but her lips parted as Heron put his palm over her mouth. She suckled slowly, her burns healing right before our eyes. The tissue regenerated, and her skin grew over strips of raw flesh, brand new and smooth.

I exhaled, able to function again when Avril's instinctive hunger kicked in, her eyes wide open as she looked up at

Heron and continued to feed on his blood. He pulled her closer so she could rest her head on his chest, and held her tight for a couple of minutes.

The smile on his face said everything. Relief washed over us all as Avril slowly recovered.

"What the hell happened?" Hansa said, still pale from everything that had just happened. She ran her fingers through her hair, then looked at Patrik with sheer befuddlement.

"I don't know." Patrik shook his head. "I did the spell perfectly, just like Viola taught me. It was supposed to work and take Avril away, not crash into the atmosphere. I can't... I don't know..."

"It nearly killed her," Jax muttered through gritted teeth, his eyes set on Avril and Heron.

"It... It was going smoothly up there," Avril managed, gently pushing Heron's hand away from her bloody lips. He didn't let go of her, though. He stayed down there, his arms wrapped around her and his head resting on top of hers. His pained expression wasn't something I'd thought I'd ever see on Heron. I had a feeling there was more beneath his playful façade, at least where Avril was concerned. I was even willing to bet that he was into her.

I waved the thought away, refocusing on the bigger problem. The interplanetary spell didn't work.

"Then, as soon as it reached the atmosphere," Avril continued, her voice weak as her body continued to mend itself, "it started buzzing a little too loud, and then... it... it just blew up..."

A minute went by as we all processed the outcome of our attempt at leaving Neraka. It didn't look good. And I sure as hell wasn't ready to endorse another attempt at the swamp witches' interplanetary spell.

"Does this... Does this mean we can't leave Neraka?" Caia croaked, looking at each of us with a hopeful expression, as if waiting for someone to tell her the opposite.

"I don't know." Hansa sighed. "I don't think so... Damn it, this isn't right! Telluris isn't working! The interplanetary spell isn't working! We're completely cut off from Calliope!"

"We can't risk another attempt, either," Jax added. "It's risky, and, by the looks of it, it might have something to do with Neraka's atmosphere. It will most likely yield the same result, or worse."

"So what do we do?" I asked, feeling my blood pressure rise.

"I'm not sure," Jax murmured. "This wasn't exactly part of the plan."

"You mean to tell me we're stuck here?" Caia asked, visibly infuriated. Her chest moved up and down with each angry breath.

"There's something really shady going on here," Heron hissed, then pointed at the upper levels of Azure Heights. "And these bastards have something to do with it, for sure!"

"Yeah, it really doesn't make sense," Patrik groaned,

pressing his fingers against his temples to relieve some of the tension. "We were able to get here using the interplanetary spell, but now we can't get out."

"Maybe it has something to do with the asteroid belt?" Scarlett offered a potential source for our woes. We all looked up, glaring at the shimmering string of purple celestial bodies cutting through the night sky. The second moon was slowly coming up, casting its amber light over us.

"I wouldn't exclude the asteroid belt. But Rewa was able to get out when she came to us for help. This doesn't make sense..." Patrik's eyebrow rose.

"Seriously, what do we do?" I asked, unable to get my own brain to function and produce some viable options. This was getting even weirder, and I hadn't even thought it was possible.

Hansa opened her mouth to say something, but a sky-splitting bang erupted from above. My instincts went into overdrive. My muscles jumped and turned to stone as I looked up. Massive fires erupted from the top level, bright orange blossoms consuming everything in their path.

"Crap," I breathed, my hands instinctively clutching my swords.

The entire top floor, the Five Lords' mansions—it was all engulfed in fire, tall flames that licked at the sky and sent black columns of smoke billowing. People screamed. An alarm went off, a constant wail that made my blood freeze.

This was all too sudden. The first question that flashed

through my brain was: did it have anything to do with what had just happened to Avril? Or was this something else entirely, with *extremely* odd timing? I'd thought I was done with the increasing weirdness and turns of events here, but... I had been wrong. I didn't even have time to properly process this.

Imen and Maras alike tumbled down the stairs, some set alight by the greedy blaze.

The Five Lords... Caspian...

"Let's go," Hansa breathed, and ran up the main alley.

We followed, leaving Heron and Avril behind—she needed a bit more time to recover. The Correction Officers from the infirmary came with us, the horror on their faces almost heartbreaking. Their Lords were up there.

I ran fast, shooting up the stairs and alleys with a thundering heart struggling in my chest.

Caspian was up there.

37

HARPER

(DAUGHTER OF HAZEL & TEJUS)

W e reached the top level just as a second explosion burst from the Kifo mansion. The screams were unbearable, as there were dozens of Imen and Maras still inside, burning alive. I pulled my hood over my head to get some protection from the blaze, and ran across the front terrace.

The others spread out and helped get as many Imen and Maras away from the fire as they could. There must have been some kind of gathering in one of the mansions, based on the number of people present. The smell of burnt wood and flesh invaded my nostrils and turned my stomach upside down.

I used my True Sight to briefly scan the mansions—all five were engulfed in high flames, the windows broken and parts of the walls ruptured where the explosions had torn through. The sound of the inferno consuming everything inside came out in rumbling crackles, a spine-chilling background to the screams of those still inside.

Caia used her fae ability to draw water from the white marble fountain still standing in the middle of the terrace, but it wasn't enough. She could only conjure brief sheets of water, which she threw at the houses.

Patrik muttered a spell and managed to draw out more, generating five thick columns of water, which he shot at the mansions, systematically tackling the fires on a local level. It still wasn't enough, but it helped Jax, Hansa, Scarlett, Fiona, and Blaze with the rescue of several Imen trapped on the lower floors.

I couldn't see Caspian anywhere, but his residence was nearly obliterated. Based on the damage alone, his mansion had been the source of both explosions. I saw Emilian running down the stairs of the Xunn house, with Rewa unconscious in his arms. He dodged falling chunks of burning wood and slabs from the ceiling.

The staircase collapsed, and they both fell through.

"Caia, give me some water cover!" I shouted, and ran toward the Xunn mansion.

She quickly shifted a stream over my head, enough to keep the flames at bay as I flashed through the broken front door and reached Emilian and Rewa. They were both injured but still alive, trapped under pieces of debris.

Scarlett joined me, and pulled Rewa out first. She carried her outside while I handled Emilian, who groaned from the pain. I caught a glimpse of his back and saw the severe burns through his tattered suit.

We made it back to the fountain, where Scarlett washed Rewa's face with water, shaking her back into consciousness.

Rowan and Vincent escaped from their mansion, along with Arrah and two more servants. Farrah was brought out by Jax, while Hansa carried her two young sons in her arms as they ran over to the edge.

Correction Officers and Mara nurses had already gathered by the stone steps with first-aid supplies, blankets, and gallons of Mara blood in wooden jugs to assist the victims. Many of the Imen who escaped from the fire had already died. Others cried as they covered them with white sheets. Blood stuck to the fabric, blossoming in heartbreaking shades of crimson.

"I need some help here!" Blaze shouted as he emerged from the Kifo mansion with Caspian.

My heart skipped a beat at the sight of him. He was unconscious as Blaze carried him out and brought him over to the fountain. He laid Caspian on the ground, and I left Emilian's side to kneel next to him. A nurse took care of Lord Obara, while Caia and Patrik continued to put out the flames and the rest of my team managed to rescue a few more people.

I applied pressure to Caspian's chest with both hands, as I couldn't hear his heartbeat.

"Come on," I muttered, beads of sweat trickling down my face.

He coughed as he regained consciousness. I bit into my palm and thrust it in front of him.

"That's it," I said, my voice trembling. "Drink, Caspian... You'll be okay..."

His lips touched my palm, and I couldn't help but shudder. He drew blood, greedily sucking as his teeth grazed my skin. I held his head up. He blinked a few times, breathing heavily. Warmth filled my ribcage and expanded into my stomach as I watched him recover, the burns on his arms and legs healing fast.

"Thank you," he rasped, then pulled himself to a sitting position.

"It's okay, you did the same for me," I said softly, unable to recognize my own voice until I understood exactly how incredibly relieved I was to see him again, and alive.

His gaze clouded as he looked at me, and his knuckles brushed against my cheek in a fleeting gesture of affection that made me tremble.

"Daddy!" Rewa's scream pierced through the fabric of this disaster.

She'd fallen to her knees, her face covered in soot. Tears streamed down her cheeks. Scarlett held her close, giving me a wary look over her shoulder.

"Darius didn't make it out of there," she said.

Gasps erupted from the remaining Lords, who were sipping Mara blood as the nurses wiped their faces with wet cloths.

"Daddy, no!" Rewa's wails were gut wrenching and raw, and I couldn't help but feel her grief, as a daughter.

Blaze ran back inside the Xunn mansion, as he was virtually impervious to fire, while Caia and Patrik continued battling the shrinking inferno across the top level of the city. Avril and Heron joined us, helping carry more victims out as Jax, Hansa, and Fiona rescued the last survivors they could find. Darius wasn't among them.

Caspian slowly leaned into me, his shoulder against mine, gradually recovering from his injuries. Farrah, Rowan, and Emilian came over, wrapped in blankets, as they, too, were healing. They were pale and distraught, tears glazing their eyes as they glanced at Rewa, who kept watching and waiting, crying her heart out. Scarlett held her close.

Blaze came out emptyhanded. Rewa doubled over, her forehead touching the cobblestone as she broke down completely. This was a tragedy unfolding at a rapid pace. And no one seemed to grasp its devastation, as shock silenced everyone, including the thousands of Maras and Imen who had gathered below.

The wounded Imen were carried downstairs to the infirmary, while the surviving Maras recovered once they had blood from their fellow citizens.

"What happened?" Jax asked, joining our side along with Hansa. They were both black with soot and ashes, their hair a little burnt and a sheet of sweat covering their faces. Hansa was worse, her wide eyes filled with tears and her hands trembling. Past the initial shock, I realized then that Hansa was experiencing terrible flashbacks from the Red Tribe massacre. Her pain poured out in ripples of red and orange.

"I... I don't know," Emilian mumbled, still processing everything. His gaze darted around.

"We were all in our homes," Farrah breathed. "Just an ordinary evening. Darius was having some friends over for dinner, as far as I know..."

"Then the explosion," Rowan sobbed, struggling to keep it together. "It started from the Xunn mansion, and it was so powerful, it burst all the way through our homes. The ground shook. The windows broke, and the fire spread so fast... so fast..."

"This was a vicious attack," Emilian said, gritting his teeth. "I don't know who perpetrated it, or why... But this was evil! It was unnatural, and... and Darius..."

I got up to get a better look at the mansions, all burnt almost entirely. The upper floors were still collapsing, piles of rubble spilling out onto the terrace as dust and black smoke billowed and thickened the air around.

The fires died down eventually, and Correction Officers started combing all residences for bodies. I could see some from where I stood, charred remains crumpled beneath burnt wood beams and slabs of stone. I'd never seen something so horrific, so... heartbreaking.

Caspian stood, straightening his back. I heard his spine crack in the process, and I looked at him. Anger poured out of him. Confusion. Grief. His hand rested on my hip for a moment, his eyes finding mine.

"I don't know what happened," he whispered, as if trying to make sure that I believed him. Since when did it matter what I thought of him?

"I believe you." I nodded slowly.

Two of the Correction Officers came out of the Xunn residence—or its remains, anyway—carrying the carbonized remains of what looked like an adult male. Something glimmered on his finger, a golden ring with precious gems, melted into the bone.

They brought him over, grief pulling their brows together as they lowered their heads and put the body down.

"That's... That's his Lordship ring," Rewa cried. "That's Daddy's ring... That... That's Daddy..."

Scarlett did her best to comfort the young Mara girl, but the poor soul was inconsolable. She'd just lost her father.

"Darius... Darius is dead," Emilian murmured, then raised his voice for the rest of the people around and below to hear. "Darius of House Xunn, one of the Five Lords of Azure Heights, was murdered!"

Gasps and sobs erupted from the crowd as the tragic news set in. Maras and Imen hugged one another, crying, grieving the loss of one of their leaders. I fought back tears as I watched the entire scene. It was impossible not to feel their pain, not to feel invested when witnessing such a tragedy. Whoever had done this, they had aimed for maximum damage and loss of life. They didn't care who got hurt or killed.

My mind kept rushing back to what had just happened to Avril, as well. Though the two incidents didn't seem connected—except, perhaps, by the horrible timing—I couldn't help but wonder whether the daemons had something to do with both. After all, they did have swamp witch magic. But to what extent? How much did they possess, to be able to destroy an interplanetary spell? This was something I was determined to address with Patrik once we got a minute with just our team. I wasn't connecting the dots just yet, but they seemed awfully close the more I thought about it.

"We are all truly sorry for your losses," Jax said. Hansa stood silent behind him. "This is the tragic result of a heinous act, and, rest assured, you have our full support in investigating this. We will help you bring the criminal... or criminals to justice."

Emilian wiped back his tears and gave Jax a polite nod,

then stared at Rewa. She inched closer to her father's body, her hands reaching out, her fingers trembling, as she wasn't sure how to touch him. Scarlett whispered something in her ear, and Rewa, through her grief and pain, nodded and sat back, leaning against her.

"You mentioned it started from the Xunn mansion," I said.

"Yes," Farrah replied.

"Judging by the damage, the Xunn mansion was the hot point." Blaze looked over his shoulder, briefly analyzing the remains of Darius's house.

"It would be fair to assume that perhaps he was the intended target?" I shrugged, glancing at Jax for feedback. It made sense in my head, based on everything I'd learned about arson during my GASP training. We'd held special sessions on extremist attacks, arson, and murder as part of our induction.

"Could it be daemon-related?" Fiona chimed in. "Whoever blew up the tunnel on the east side of the mountain wanted me separated from Hansa. They wanted me to reach the prison. Daemons attacked the prison. I'm just trying my luck at an educated guess here..."

"Someone blew up the gorge earlier today, as well," I added. "Whoever did it wanted to break us away from the Correction Officers. Then... daemons attacked."

"I wouldn't exclude it as a possibility, but we'll need to

do a thorough investigation," Jax replied, then glanced over his shoulder at Hansa. "What do you think?"

Hansa was still reeling from everything that had happened. The pain emanating from her was impossible to describe, and I didn't want to mention it out loud, either. She valued her image as a strong succubus, and everything she was experiencing in that moment pointed to a weakness she never would've wanted to display in front of strangers.

"Jax, we should definitely discuss this later, after all the bodies are cleared out and we can plan our resources," I said, trying to draw attention away from Hansa. "This is an unexpected turn, and we need to rethink our strategy now."

"Yeah, especially since we can't leave this damn place," Heron muttered, keeping himself close to Avril.

Caspian gave me a surprised look.

"What do you mean, you can't leave?" he asked, his voice low and husky.

"The interplanetary spell didn't work," Patrik replied. "Neraka's atmosphere rejected it for no apparent reason."

"That's not right." Emilian frowned, scratching his beard with trembling fingers. "Rewa was able to leave... You were able to come in... It doesn't make sense."

"Tell me about it," Avril muttered, her arms crossed over her chest. "I nearly got killed when the spell tried to reach space. It exploded."

Farrah then gasped, covering her mouth with her hands.

"Oh, dear, that's what that flash was," she said. "I saw it from my bedroom window…"

A minute passed as we all stared at each other.

Whether we liked it or not, we were stuck here. Someone had managed to kill Darius by blowing the entire top level up. The daemons were far better organized than we'd initially given them credit for. And there were still so many questions left unanswered from before. It was as if Neraka were deliberately toying with us, testing our limits and playing with our heads—when it wasn't trying to kill us.

"Either way, GASP will start sending people after us soon," Jax said. "We've been gone for three days now, and they've yet to hear from us. Surely they must be rounding up the troops now. We might see them as soon as tomorrow."

"But until then, we need to stay alert and keep doing our jobs," Patrik added. "We have to expand the city protection spell to its underground. Do you know if the tunnels have been sealed, Lord Kifo?"

"I was waiting for Cadmus to come up and confirm, but I haven't seen him yet," Caspian replied, then glanced around with a concerned expression, as if hoping to see Cadmus somewhere.

"We need to get back to the infirmary," I said. "The protection spell satchels are down there."

"Right, first things first." Jax nodded. "Caia and Blaze, take Patrik with you to the infirmary and follow his instructions with regards to planting the satchels in the prison. I'm sure one of Lord Kifo's Correction Officers will guide you to it from the city, since we're assuming the tunnels are sealed."

"Absolutely," Caspian replied, and snapped his fingers. One of his guards moved forward from the crowd, waiting for Caia, Blaze, and Patrik.

"Fiona, you know what you have to do as well, I suppose." Jax raised an eyebrow.

"Yup," she replied, and joined Patrik's side.

"The rest of us need to talk," Jax continued, then looked at Caspian. "Can you have your Correction Officers clear this level and keep everyone away? This is a crime scene now. We can't have anyone tamper with evidence."

Caspian agreed and motioned for his guards to usher people off the edge of the terrace and away from the stone stairs. I glanced at the mansion ruins, while Vincent helped Rewa up and guided her away from Darius's remains.

"I'm sure the White Star Hotel below will accommodate us," Vincent said slowly, his arm around Rewa's shoulders. "We'll go make the arrangements now."

With everything that had happened, my nerves were stretched beyond their limits. More questions and a crippled trust between us and the Exiled Maras were the defining factors of our current circumstances. On top of that, we had soul-eating daemons prowling around the city, and thousands of innocent Maras and Imen as potential victims, with hundreds already missing or dead.

It felt like we were swimming upstream, and I feared where this salmon run would lead. GASP couldn't come soon enough.

I turned to find Caspian staring at me, his jade gaze dark and soft. In that moment, at least, all I could feel was relief. Relief that Blaze had managed to get to him in time. Relief that he was still alive. The reasons for my relief were mixed and... complicated, and I didn't have the energy to sort through them right now. There was one my mind could settle on, however:

He owed me an answer.

38

DRAVEN

The early morning sun rose lazily over Mount Zur, its golden rays bathing the terrace outside in a warm light. I was the first in the council room, so I pulled the window shutters down and turned the lights on, instead, preparing for the others' arrival. Derek, Tejus, and Lawrence had agreed to meet with Field, Serena, and me to go over our last conversation with Hansa.

We'd watched our GASP team leave for Neraka only yesterday just before noon. I knew Serena worried about Harper, but she'd managed to relax a little after Hansa's updates. They were all okay, and actively investigating the disappearances in Azure Heights.

There was something still bugging me, a sliver of doubt that I was unable to identify. As if something felt off. But I couldn't put my finger on it. I sat down, resting my hands on the table as I closed my eyes.

I took a deep breath. Day two of the Neraka investigative mission, and we'd just reached the six-hour mark. It was time to reach out and check in with the team.

"Telluris Hansa!" I called out.

There it was again—that little nudge that didn't feel right. I couldn't sense Hansa's soul at all. I couldn't sense any of their souls. This connection was meant to be flawless, altogether resistant to time and space.

A buzz emerged in the back of my head, reminding me of Field and Jovi's radio communicators whenever they switched frequencies.

"Telluris Hansa!" I tried again.

Several seconds went by, during which time a knot quietly shaped in my stomach.

"Draven!" Her voice came through.

"Are you okay?" I asked.

"Yes, yes, I'm fine. We all are. Just enjoying breakfast here at the inn," she replied, seemingly in a good mood. "The food is fantastic, by the way!"

Since when does Hansa care about food?

"How is the investigation going?" I asked.

"It's slow, but there's definitely something fishy going on here," Hansa said, her voice muffled. "We're going to study the Valley of Screams after lunch again. Caia and Blaze are still doing some interviews. We don't know what's causing the disappearances, but there are suspicions of strange animals lurking in the gorges that might be linked to this. We didn't find anything during last night's expedition, so we want to try an analysis under daylight, for now."

"Are there any traces? Perhaps Avril can track a scent?"

"Yes, that's one avenue we're exploring," she replied. "But we're also... look... may... Maras... if they..."

Her voice began cutting out, like a bad radio transmission.

"Hansa? Hansa, can you hear me?" I called out.

I couldn't hear her anymore. That knot in my stomach twisted itself into a painful position. I didn't like this at all. I sighed, then thought I'd try another team member instead.

"Telluris Jaxxon!" I chanted.

A few seconds later, his familiar voice echoed in my head.

"Draven," he responded. "I can't hear you very well."

"Yeah, I can tell. I was just talking to Hansa when the conversation dropped," I replied, slightly irritated, pinching the bridge of my nose. "Telluris isn't supposed to work like this."

"I understand," he said calmly. "Maybe it has something to do with the asteroid belt."

"It shouldn't. Telluris links souls. It doesn't answer to space and matter in any way."

"I don't know what else to tell you." Jax sighed. "I can hear you better now. It probably *is* affected by distance or the asteroids somehow. Maybe the Druids who devised this spell were wrong. Who knows?"

"Maybe," I muttered, unsatisfied by the way my stomach reacted to Telluris's instability. "Anyway. I understand you're going to the Valley of Screams today?"

"Yes, in two to three hours, depending on when Caia and Blaze get back from the interviews," Jax replied.

"What can you tell me about the Five Lords of Azure Heights?"

"They're nice and hospitable," Jax said. "They seem like nice people, but I can't yet clear them of everything. Blame it on my people's old grudge against the Exiled Maras, but I've yet to give them my vote of confidence. Their society seems well tied together, and the Imen seem okay with living among them. Technically speaking, I have no reason to distrust them right now, besides ancient bad blood."

"I understand. Have they given you any reason to be suspicious of them?"

"None whatsoever. Like I said, it's probably just the old family grudge I'm trying to shake off. My grandfather, Shadow, carried his anger into his grave."

"I was telling Hansa to maybe consider having Avril use her tracking skills to pick up a scent in the city, regarding the disappearances." I changed the topic.

"Yes, I'll make sure she comes with us to the scene of the last disappearance," he replied. "She'll sniff something out for sure. Listen, Draven, we need to go now. Our guide for the gorges is here, we need to study the gorge maps with him. Let's catch up in six hours."

I exhaled sharply, then leaned against the back of my chair.

"That's fine, I'll speak to you then," I said, my tone brisk. "Just be careful out there."

"We will, don't worry. We have a dragon, remember?"

I could almost hear the smile in his voice before the silence settled over me. Perhaps I was overreacting and I had no reason to worry so much about Telluris. Maybe Jax was right and the spell was, in fact, affected by the distance. There were few accounts of Telluris being used outside our galaxy, after all. I could do myself a favor and check them out in the Druid Archive, just in case. They could shed more light on the spell's behavior.

The door opened. Serena walked in, lighting me up on the inside like the morning sun. Her father, Tejus, great-grandfather Derek, and Lawrence and Field followed, each giving me a brief smile and nod before they took their seats at the table.

"Have you heard from them yet?" Serena asked, taking her seat next to me.

"Just now, actually." I nodded and squeezed her hand in mine.

"Any news? How is the investigation going?" Tejus pressed.

"So far, nothing new," I muttered. "They're checking the

Valley of Screams again later. They didn't get anything out of it last night."

I briefed them about the rest of my conversations with Hansa and Jax, careful to also include the communication glitches. They all agreed it most likely had something to do with the distance or the asteroid belt. Or both.

It did help to hear them say something I'd been contemplating since yesterday, but I still couldn't get rid of that knot in my stomach. I figured I'd go ahead and check those Druid Archives later, just to get some peace of mind.

In the meantime, I was already looking forward to the next check-in. I decided I'd reach out to Patrik or Harper directly, just to see if I had the same issues with them.

Until then, however, I could only hope that our team would come through and unravel the Nerakian mystery sooner rather than later. I really wasn't comfortable with them all the way over there. I knew it was part of GASP's operation, but still... Neraka irked me a little.

There's something about it... Something just doesn't feel right.

READY FOR THE NEXT PART OF THE SHADIANS' STORY?

Dear Shaddict,

Thank you for reading A Hunt of Fiends.

The next book in the series, **ASOV 54: A Den of Tricks** releases **January 6th, 2018**!

Things are about to get wild...

Visit www.bellaforrest.net to order your copy.

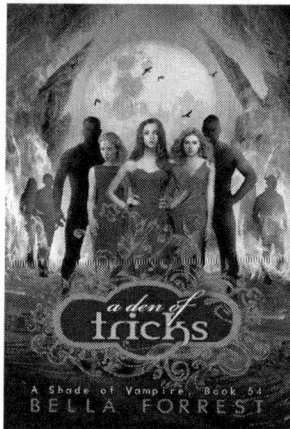

Have a fantastic holiday season, and I'll see you in January!

Love,

Bella x

P.S. Join my VIP email list and I'll send you a personal reminder as soon as I have a new book out. Visit here to sign up: **www.forrestbooks.com**

(Your email will be kept 100% private and you can unsubscribe at any time.)

P.P.S. Follow The Shade on Instagram and check out some of the beautiful graphics: @ashadeofvampire

You can also come say hi on Facebook: www.facebook.com/AShadeOfVampire

And Twitter: @ashadeofvampire

Made in the USA
Lexington, KY
09 December 2017